I0588424

althea gyles

A WOMAN
WITHOUT A SOUL
AND OTHER WRITINGS

edited by
daniel corrick

and with an appendix by
aleister crowley

THIS IS A SNUGGLY BOOK

Introduction and Collection Copyright © 2024
by Daniel Corrick.
All rights reserved.

ISBN: 978-1-64525-158-3

A WOMAN
WITHOUT A SOUL
AND OTHER WRITINGS

ALTHEA GYLES (1867-1949), was a poet and artist, whose illustrations adorned books by the likes of Oscar Wilde and Ernest Dowson. An acquaintance of Aleister Crowley, who called her the "wickedest man in the world", and the lover of the "decadent" publisher Leonard Smithers, she was a member of Hermetic Order of the Golden Dawn, before proceeding down other paths. Her illustrations and verse appeared in numerous magazines, such as the *Saturday Review*, *Kensington*, and the theosophical magazine *Orpheus*.

DANIEL CORRICK is an editor and literary historian with a specialist interest in nineteenth-century literature, especially the evolution of Gothicism and the Decadent movement. He has worked on a number of volumes including the collected fiction of Montague Summers, and unpublished works of Edgar Saltus and Edward Heron-Allen. In addition, he has edited several anthologies, including *Drowning in Beauty: The Neo-Decadent Anthology* (Snuggly Books, 2018).

CONTENTS

INTRODUCTION

ALTHEA GYLES is seldom remembered beyond occasional mentions as an Irish artist or a woman of the *fin de siècle*, yet had it not been for the malice of Fate her illustrations and book designs could easily have come to be as representative of the Decadent movement as those of Aubrey Beardsley. Her art, both visual and literary, is informed by the ideas and personalities of some of the major 1890s figures, most of whom she knew and who thought highly of her work. More so this oeuvre was the product of a deeply held belief that by craft and imagination one could come to know and better participate in the hidden order of the universe, a belief that involved her in the conflicts of that most famous of nineteenth century secret societies: the Hermetic Order of the Golden Dawn. Until now her most interesting writing has remained unpublished, shown only through tantalising quotes in scholarly articles. This volume collects together a representative sample of her shorter fiction and poems, along with presenting a brief introduction to her life and works.

Althea, born Margaret Alethea Gyles, was the youngest of three sisters. There is some confusion about the exact date of her birth but we do know she was born in January of 1867, in Bath, Somerset. From an early age she showed a passion for drawing, which soon took on something of a religious calling after she was exposed to the symbolic, highly spiritualised view of art associated with the later Pre-Raphaelites. Her family moved to Dublin in 1899, shortly after which the young Althea broke contact with them following a quarrel with her father, supposedly over her desire to turn her artistic inclinations into a carrier, leaving home determined to make a name for herself. For several months she undertook artistic training at a school but, unused to and unprepared for the challenges of financial independence, soon found herself in a state of abject poverty.

Through a stroke of luck Gyles met the leader of the Dublin Theosophical Society, E.J. Dick, who offered her lodgings in his house in nearby Ely Street, then serving as a kind of commune for mystically minded students and artists. The group shared no set doctrine;

the prevailing intellectual climate being an inchoate mixture of Hermeticism and various theories of reincarnation drawn from Eastern philosophy; these, however, would prove a formative influence on Gyles, raised as she was in an atmosphere of proprietorial Anglo-Protestantism. It was here that she became acquainted with the young William Butler Yeats, who recognised the potential of her drawings and the almost fanatical ardour with which she executed them. Unfortunately, he also noticed in her a self-destructive dissatisfaction which would torment her throughout her life and lead to so many works being left unfinished. After an argument with some of the other housemates, Gyles departed, briefly taking a room in Mountpleasant Square where she wrote the novella, "A Woman Without a Soul", one of the characters of which would prove eerily prescient.

Around this time there occurred some form of reconciliation between Gyles and her family, who subsequently paid for her to continue her studies at Slade School of Art. In 1892 she moved to London, where she re-established contact with Yeats, and over the next few years became a recognised figure in Bohemian circles, rhapsodic in her idealistic views on poetry and art. Her appearance added something to this growing mystique; tall, pale, with red gold hair and long tapering fingers she resembled one of Burne-Jones' celestial maidens. Upon meeting her shortly afterwards, Oscar Wilde was allegedly so charmed by her demeanour that he treated her to a series of meals based on the colours of her garments, an act of affectionate whimsy that won him her fanatical loyalty. Her London circle included Ernest Dawson, Arthur Symonds, and the publisher Leonard Smithers, with whom she was later to have a short-lived, disastrous affair.

It was in collaboration with Yeats, however, that Gyles was destined to reach her intellectual and artistic heights. Her designs feature on three of his books—*The Secret Rose*, *Poems*, and *The Wind Among the Reeds*—there representing an intricate intermarrying of text and visual art influenced by the complex synthesis of Western occultism that was the ceremonial magic of the Golden Dawn. If the enthusiasm for such appears credulous to us now it must be remembered that they were no less far-fetched than many of the enthusiasms which gripped the post-war generation, like the oxymoronically named Dialectical Materialism or the apophatic mysticism of Wittgenstein's *Tractatus*. For all its Egyptian trappings and hat tips to Theosophy's Orientalism, the language of the Golden Dawn was rooted in the mysticism of the Kabballah and alchemical symbolism retrospectively associated with the semi-mythical Rosicrucians. It was that language which Gyles would apply in crisp Art Nouveau calligraphy; her cover of *Poems* features a central rose and cross motif from which issue forth a spiral of seed-bearing vines, whilst that of *The Secret Rose* shows a slain knight from whose loins sprout a stylised rose arbour in the form of the Kabbalistic Tree of Life. Yeats was to recognise and praise her achievements in his essay "A Symbolic Artist and the Coming of Symbolic Art."

Although Gyles was never a formal member of the Golden Dawn, her friendship with Yeats led her to play an unwitting part in one of the most infamous and bizarre feuds of the 1890s. As part of the clique of artists who frequented the Café Royal she gained a passing acquaintance with one Aleister Crowley, who at the time was facing expulsion from the Order on the basis of sexually predatory behaviour and alleged experiments with black magic. She visited him on occasion at his Chancery Lane lodgings to chat about esoteric subjects; however, during these visits, Crowley came to believe that Gyles was responsible for furnishing his then nemesis Yeats with stolen personal effects for use in rites of sympathetic magic, which saw him subject to nightly attacks from a vampiric dream entity. In retaliation he played a trick on her which involved a skeleton, real or artificial, falling into her lap unexpectedly from a cupboard. A few years later, with typical literary bombast, Crowley immortalised the event in a short story "At the Fork of the Roads", in which the vapid Hypatia Gay (Gyles) serves as a pawn of the "lank melancholy unwashed poet" and "dabbler in magic" William Bute (Yeats) in his demonic campaign against the generally superlative, not to mention "royally Celtic", Count Swanoff (Crowley). With the help of another magician (Crowley's mentor Allan Bennett), the demon is slain and Bute defeated, in the process of which Hypatia offers herself willing to "bestial worms of the Slime" and thence "a Bond Street publisher", the latter of which is presented as the more heinous transgression against sexual and metaphysical decency.[1]

Despite what some online sources say there is little evidence to suggest that Gyles ever had a romantic relationship with Crowley; none of the primary sources hint at this and neither Yeats' scholar and the author of the first schol-

---

[1] Crowley himself had other reasons for disliking Smithers, considering that the latter had recently accepted both manuscript and payment for the printing of Crowley's second collection of verse, *Green Alps*, only later to claim that all the proofs had been destroyed in a fire around the time of his bankruptcy, an account the occultist was rightly sceptical about.

arly account of Gyles' career Ian Fletcher, nor Richard Elleman, who published Crowley's own account of his involvement with her and Yeats as recounted several months before his death, mention any form of sexual intimacy between the two of them. Crowley's biographers make no mention of it, save for speculating that sexual jealousy may have proved one of the motives for depicting Gyles in such lights. The assumption appears to have arisen from a line in Elleman's article to the effect that Gyles was "forced to give way entirely to his baleful fascination," which in the context meant (allegedly) confessing to Yeats' supposed malefic misdeeds. Indeed, given the Irish poet's condemnatory reaction to her relationship with Smithers it is unlikely he would have remained silent on any supposed liaison with the man he feared risked turning the Golden Dawn into a reformatory.

Gyles' all too real relationship with Leonard Smithers occurred in 1899 and lasted for about a year. Although a *bon viveur* and generous when the mood took him, the publisher's increasingly dishonest business practices and enthusiasm for sexually explicit material in the wake of Wilde's trial led many to avoid him. Yeats thought him a drunken brute and forbade her to bring him with her on visits. It is possible that Smithers also looked to Gyles as a replacement for the recently deceased Beardsley. At his bequest she produced cover designs for Ernest Dowson's *Decorations* and a black and white frontispiece for John White-Rodyng's play *The Night*. More important were a series of five drawings she did for a luxury presentation of Wilde's poem, "The Harlot's House," depicting in silhouette a bacchanal of sinuous female forms and horned skeletons interlaced. Along with winning her compliments from the exiled Wilde, it is, along with a piece Yeats included in his essay entitled "Lilith," one of the few instances in her work which depict wickedness as opposed to sanctity.

It is unknown what lead to the collapse of Gyles' relationship with Smithers, but various chroniclers imply that her failure to prevail on her wealthy family to aid him in the face of looming bankruptcy was a factor.

By the end of 1899 distress and a serious though undiagnosed health problem precipitated a breakdown on Gyles' part leading to long periods in sanatoriums and medical spas over the next two years. Yeats aided her by concealing many of her books and papers during a visit from bailiffs, but a heated argument in the course of which he took the side of the inhabitants of a spa with whom Gyles had quarrelled led to a rapid cooling in their friendship. In an attempt to relieve the poverty ill-health brought her, Arthur Symonds arranged for Thomas Mosher to publish a collection of Gyles' poems, which fell through at the last moment because she would not remove the dedication "To the Beautiful Memory of Oscar Wilde," the publisher having objected only to the word "beautiful." This peculiar tendency for self-sabotage *in extremis* would repeat itself five years later when a similar collection was to be published by Grant & Richards, only for it to be ultimately rejected due to her refusal to correct the proofs or allow others to do so.

The early part of the twentieth century was a climb out of ill-health and poverty into a more comfortable situation. Though Gyles never achieved the same iconic success as she did with the designs for Yeats' volumes she re-mained productive. She abandoned the risqué elements associated with Smithers' publica-tions, which one feels more of a concession to fashion at any rate, and returned to a visual and literary aesthetic closer to the Arts and Crafts movement, designing an illuminated alphabet, "the Alphabet of the Wonderful Wood," after the manner of the Kelmscott Press. She became involved with the Ruskin-inspired Peasant Arts Society, endorsing some of the social causes associated with that movement, such as the primacy of handicraft over mechanical reproduction, opposition to materialistic instrumentalism and the importance of nature and beauty for improving the well-being of the urban working class. It was for this purpose she released, under the pseudonym "John Meade", the 1914 book *Letters to Children about Drawing, Painting and Something More*, which is as much about her mystical views on astrology, colour symbolism and spiritual purpose of art as it is about any formal techniques.

In the decades following the war, Gyles became viewed by the new generations as a curious link to the glamour and tragedy of the Decadents. Many were keen to meet her and even offer support, though of these latter the majority often gave up in exasperation. Amongst these new friends were numbered the writer Eleanor Farjeon, the critic Clifford Bax, then editor of the Theosophical journal *Orpheus*, and Compton and Faith Mackenzie, the latter of whom left an unflattering, albeit comic, portrayal of Gyles as a costume-jewelleryed eccentric obsessed with the memory of Wilde and Beardsley in her 1957 novel *Tatting*. At the beginning of the twenties Grant & Richards requested a memoir dealing with Gyles' experiences of the nineties; instead, she wrote and submitted a novel entitled *Pilgrimage*, a rosy aesthetic narrative about bohemian life in the Kent countryside, with a plot involving past lives and characters based on Yeats, George Russell, and the Mackenzies. It was to be her last major work. From the onset of the nineteen-thirties little is heard of her, though she may have continued writing in the form of children's stories. As the years moved on, she slipped back into obscurity, moving between squalid flats and lodging houses accompanied only by a few treasured books and mementoes. Farjeon remained a friend and some family reconciliation must have occurred, for she corresponded with her nieces. She died in a London nursing home at the age of eighty in 1949.

"A Woman Without a Soul", is the longest and most ambitious item in the present volume. From the address on the exercises books in which the story was written we know it was composed when she was twenty-five, shortly before she left Ireland for London. The exact history of those notebooks after Gyles' death is uncertain, but they were purchased by the National Library of Ireland from an antiquarian bookseller as part of a bulk lot of Yeats' materials in 1974; given that Gyles left many of her books with that poet to avoid bailiffs it might be that they were misplaced amongst his personal effects until his death, whence it passed into the hands of private collectors.

The scholar Kristin Mahoney, author of one of the few contemporary overviews of Gyles' work, describes it with some justice as a feminised retelling of Wilde's *The Picture of Dorian Gray*[2]. The influence of Wilde's novella can be seen not only in the philosophical dichotomy between internal and external beauty, but also in the aesthetics of the central scene in which the protagonist gives up her soul: here the lush, almost mystical, description of the cottage flowers and the manner in which the architect of her supernatural predication observes the flower-decked tableaux of her sleeping form "as a painter might look at a beautiful picture that he has just completed" recall the famous garden scene wherein Dorian learns the philosophy of aesthetic hedonism. There are, however, important differences in the moral dilemmas which the two stories present. The hero of Wide's novella acquires his unnatural youth and immunity to physical corruption unwittingly, as the result of a prayer answered by an inscrutable and ironic Providence; whereas Gyles' heroine, Winifred Ledbury, knowingly partakes of a Faustian bargain in order to escape the restraints of conscience and moral

---

2 Professor Mahoney discusses Gyles in her book *Literature and the Politics of Post-Victorian Decadence*. Aside from *The Picgture of Dorian Gray* another potential influence is the Wild's short story "The Fisherman and His Soul," which saw publication the same year that Gyles' wrote her novella.

responsibility. Yet despite this lack of initial culpability Dorian was never a good person, he passes from ignorance to wickedness, his death coming about not through catharsis or repentance, but as a result of fury at the evidence of his own spiritual hideous made manifest through the famous painting; whereas Winifred is cognisant of the evil she has done and its effects on others, only for love to throw her into a dilemma whereby she risks perpetuating it. With her heroine's final impasse Gyles highlights the cruel social disparity, present now as then, whereby the beauty and desirability of a woman is conventionally supposed to pass very quickly whilst men remain of eligible age for a much longer period.

In the novella's black magician villain Eugene Caruthers readers cannot help but see an eerie precursor to Crowley, right down to the gnomic quotes about knowledge and power. Although this is of course a coincidence, it is enlightening to see how such tropes we associate with the wicked Crowleyesque occultist were already present in mystically minded circles before that figure appeared on the scene. There have been attempts to link the figure of Caruthers with a Captain Roberts, an actual Dublin occultist who allegedly served as the model for the leader of the black magicians in Yeats' reminiscence, "The Sorcerers", but there is no basis for this beyond the fact that both indulge in animal sacrifice. Indeed, Gyles' character is more morally ambiguous than Yeats' sorcerer or Count Swanoff; although his actions are described as wicked and leading to tragedy they also result in potential redemption not only for Winnifred, but also for her husband. Given Gyles' Theosophical leanings, one doubts she would accord much potential for self-willed evil as opposed to sin through ignorance and misplaced appetites, and even then with the sinner serving as an unwitting instrument of Karma.

The subject of reincarnation and the ongoing struggles carried over from past lives is one of the main preoccupations of Gyles' fiction. It features in an untitled play in which the mysterious antipathy between two characters is revealed to be the result of a criminal act carried out by previous incarnations in Renaissance Italy, and in her later novel, *Pilgrimage*, where the attraction between the hero and heroine is the result of prenatal forces. In "A Woman Without a Soul" this motif is obscured by more obviously occult themes like Faustian bargains and spirits of darkest Egypt, but it provides the metaphysical schema by which the plot must be interpreted.

Gyles' later fiction is more optimistic in tone, corresponding to her increased interest in the Arts and Crafts movement and various rural religious communities, ideals which one suspects were closer in line with her original Pre-Raphaelite spiritualised vision of art than the Decadent obsession with sin and erotic transgression. She retains, however, a strong vein of Aestheticism, which she would have held was the true hallmark of *fin-de-siècle* art. Her later attempts at novels are in the manner of bohemian comedies referencing the comic as opposed to the tragic aspects of the nineties generation. More unique are the handful of fairy tales she authored in the first decades of the twentieth century, of which "Aspiration" and "A Christmas Crib" are presented here. They too owe their pedigree to Wilde, in this case the stories in *The Happy Prince* and *The House of Pomegranates*. Although intended for children they are also parables for worldly things, with "Aspiration" hinting delicately at how civilization breeds ennui and from that sadism. The reoccurring theme of the mystical Wood, not only as an abode of fauns and nymphs, but also as a plane on which humanity can undergo a kind of primordial spiritual romance, is inspired by William Morris' *Wood Beyond the Worlds*: given the similarity between it as a theme and the aborted "Alphabet of the Wonderful Wood" the two may have been linked, with the alphabet intended to illustrate these stories. The short essay "Winter", which accompanies "A Christmas Crib", sheds light on her curious belief in the presence and importance of natural elemental spirits, which also appears several times in her *Letters*. One wonders whether if she had kept to this project she might have enjoyed a second fame as a children's writer, albeit one with the unconventional goal of promoting artistic endeavour as a kind of practical white magic used to commune with elementals and past selves.

Poetry was the written medium to which Gyles felt most drawn, and she continued submitting verse for publication long after the nineties craze died. More than with the fiction her poetic subjects remain invariant throughout her life (with the exception of a sudden burst of Christmas poems written for a children's charity). The first major appearance of her verse was in 1894 when, with the encouragement of Yeats and George Russell, her poem "Dew-Time" was published in *Pall Mall Magazine* accompanied by a striking black and white illustration in the style soon to be popularised in *The Yellow Book*. The greater portion of her verse appeared over the course of the next decade in various magazines, most notably *The Saturday Review* and *The Kensington Magazine*. Among her papers there is a handwritten manuscript giving a selection of eighteen poems, presumably for potential publication—one of the pieces bears the date 1913. Her last item in a major magazine appeared in 1917.

Like Yeats, Gyles is primarily a mystical poet; her favourite themes are divine beauty and the world beyond the veil. Within this subject there is a contrast between world-weariness and glorification of holy sacrifice with varying results. Aesthicised *ennui* with life is of course a hallmark of Decadent poetry and places Gyles' verse squarely in that camp, with her closest thematic kin and possible later stylistic influence being Ernest Dawson. Of this kind are "Parma Violets," "Pierrot" (also a favourite character of Dawson's), "Romantic Landscapes", and "The Song of the Seine", the latter of which repeats the dilemma of the opening pages of "A Woman Without a Soul". Most successful are the poems "For a Sepulchre" and "From Rosamor dead to Favonius for whom she died", in which Gyles' conveys clever antonymic juxtapositions of carnal desire, personal identity, decay and spiritual love. It is unknown whether she was familiar with the verse of Emily Dickson, published the year before she left Dublin, whose love letters to death resemble her own, albeit stripped of occult imagery.

It is when appealing to that very imagery, however, that Gyles most successfully presents both something of herself and of a generation. As with her drawings, it is through the use of the motif of the mystical rose she expresses much of the essence of *fin-de-siècle* occultism, with that blossom representing higher consciousness, immorality, the blood of Christ and the alchemical union between masculine and feminine. This is of course the Rosicrucian blend of mysticism stated most explicitly in "An Old Iron Cross Wrought with Lilies and a Rose" and in "To a Band of Servers", which makes reference to that favourite object of mystical initiation, the Holy Grail. To highlight how significant this language would have been to certain persons it need only be remarked that the true name of the inner society of the Golden Dawn was "the Order of the Rose of Ruby and the Cross of Gold."

With her mysticism, informing both phrase and image, Gyles expresses a school of philosophy as important to the history of decadence as the Aestheticism of Wilde or the pessimistic Catholicism of the French *poètes maudits*. Ironically for someone whose aesthetics initially look back to Pre-Raphaelitism's idealised medievalism and who presented herself as reverential than iconoclastic Gyles' vision shares a kinship with that of Crowley himself in that the "surface elements" of Decadence, carnality and morbidity, are themselves redeemed, as opposed to washed away or forgiven, in a form of mystical apotheosis. Through all the complexities of Gyles' character, and the idiosyncrasies of her beliefs, it is when treating of this alchemy of souls both terrible and beautiful that her work is at its most successful. Theosophy provided her with the doctrine of reincarnation by which actions may echo down the hallways of birth and death, setting the scene for dramas beyond our ken, and Rosicrucianism the climax of carnal self-sacrifice and transformation by which they would end, a transcendence of Decadence by the Occult.

A NOTE ON THE TEXTS

MUCH of the material in this collection has been taken from manuscripts and typescripts, with some small errors being corrected. In the case of "A Woman Without A Soul", the original manuscript is largely unpunctuated and the editor has taken the liberty of applying punctuation in order to prepare it for print. The editor would like to thank Professor Kristin Mahoney and the staff at the University of Reading Special Collections for their kind help in making Gyles' material available.

A WOMAN
WITHOUT A SOUL
AND OTHER WRITINGS

A WOMAN WITHOUT
A SOUL

I

Oh love of my Death my life is Pain.

THE air was still with an awful stillness, the stillness of a human heart that holds its breath after a deathblow, as if the heart of nature was in unison with the daughter of hers who, with clenched hands and white face, stood amongst the shadows of the trees which grew down to the brink of the breathless pool. The only movement was the quivering of the blades of grass and the trembling of the iris flowers as they settled once more like quicksilver. The only sound the parting of the branches as a man wended his way quickly and impatiently through their luxuriance, as if glad to leave the stillness and quiet of the shade, and regain the sun-smitten roadway.

But these sounds and movements did not reach the woman's being. She heard nothing but the last words of a voice that had once whispered to her in passion-shaping accents. She felt nothing but the presence of a hand that had held hers so often in that golden week gone by, and she saw only a face—looked only into the eyes that had once made her own forget the sunlight. But now it seemed as if the words smote with intolerable pain against her brain, as if the hand was closing around her heart with torturous grip, as if the eyes that looked into hers burned like sharp flame to her very soul. And this was the end! Over and over again she heard the words, "We have had a very pleasant time together haven't we, I wish it could have lasted longer, but pleasant things must end sometimes, and—you knew I was going to be married didn't you? Well, good bye——" The sentence was not finished, all but the last words were spoken in an impatient half defiant voice, but in the end even this man's self-hardened conscience smote him with a little remorse and his world-deadened soul sense realized dimly the pain that he had voluntarily inflicted; and his fingers which had touched her hand in a formal handshake lingered around hers with the old touch, and his voice grew low with the old accents that had thrilled her through and through.

And so this man and woman parted for the last time as formally (save for their two little acts of grace) as if they had but met the day before, they, who only a week or so ago, had lingered upon their passion with locked hands and lips that spoke of meetings on the morrow; and gradually, to the woman's stunned tears, did love now clad in memory's garments show these things, and a look of wild terror and despair grew and deepened in her eyes. She stood as one who has received a death sentence, then suddenly, with a cry of unutterable despair, she parted her white lips, "Oh, my love! my love!" she cried, "I have lost you! If only death had parted us I could have borne it, but that you should love another woman! another woman! another woman!" she kept repeating the words over and over again with half-frenzied reiteration. "No, it cannot be that—after all he—after—oh I could bear the separation if only—if only he had left me the memory of the old looks and words, but now this last parting will come forever between me and them—I cannot bear it!"

She stepped suddenly to the brink of the dark silent pool. The wild briar roses clung to her dress as if they would fain hold her back, the stiff leaves of the yellow irises seemed raised as a feeble barrier to bar her progress. She stepped on the brink for a moment, just for one moment that she might speak his name.

"Hubert, my love," she murmured, "I have loved you so, so much that we must meet again someday."

But in the confines of the bleak space Love stood revealed and pleaded with her against herself, and she waited and looked not into the dark waters of the pool below, but into her own life and saw a deeper darkness there, a shrieking whirlpool, and her soul saw in the darkness a relief from the flames that surrounded it.

"No, no," she cried, "I cannot! I cannot! No—not live for his sake, I cannot live when life is torture, when every thought burns like flame. Oh Love!" she cried as if she saw and heard him there. "Do not ask me to do this when you have made my life Hell, do not bid me live, you will not be so cruel, only," she murmured "if this should harm him, if this should lay a sin upon his soul! His soul! Oh God!" she cried aloud, grasping the willow tree behind her as if to restrain herself by force. "The misery this knowledge of a soul brings, if only I could rid myself of mine for a moment I could feel peace in Death."

"You wanted me I think," said a voice behind her. It was a voice that mingled in harmony with her thoughts and met her like a friend in that twilit borderland between Life and Death in which she was standing irresolute, and, as a drowning man catches at the hand held out to save him, so this woman flung herself on the ground before her and caught the hand of the speaker in hers.

"Oh save me! oh help me!" she cried, "help me to die now, rid me of my soul if only for an instant that I may kill myself. I call it torture—torture!"

"Peace," cried the stranger looking down on the white upturned face with its wild beseeching eyes; it was of one who loved and fought some desperate battle against one stronger than themselves, the face of a strong woman who had found how weak she was in the hands of Fate. But something in the face thrilled Eugene Caruthers through and through, it was as if a glorious price was held forth for his winning and he accepted the challenge with eagerness.

"That is not very difficult to do," he said in a soft melodious voice, "but you must come to my house."

"Yes, yes," she cried, "only come quickly— quickly every moment seems a lifetime."

She sped swiftly before him, half running, at intervals he saw her white dress gleaming through the trees and at such turns of the winding path that lead through the wood he found her standing waiting, with eager eyes and imploring hands asking him to follow quickly.

He did not hasten but followed her musing as he went, "I am very fortunate," he murmured, "I did not think this would come so soon, it is a relief after the hard study of the past two years to have some work like this, I knew distinctly when I saw her with that man this would follow, I vaguely remember him somewhere, somehow, where was it," he was speaking half aloud rather as if he were asking someone else.

"Oh yes," letting his head sink with an abrupt characteristic movement he continued his meditations, "I am glad I watched this from the commencement, let's see," he said, opening the volume of *The Book of Ratziel* that he held under his arm and taking some note papers on which he had written notes and signs and fragments of words in indecipherable dialects. "They have met before that is certain—that is what drew him here—her soul has precisely struggled with him through several lives, it seems that in this incarnation both her material and spiritual attraction to this man are equally strong, as long as they remain so this struggle will continue. But I think, I hope, this time that they are nearer. I feel this life holds the crisis—she feels it too, she feels the need of some supreme effort; her two natures have by their previous struggles gained unusual strength for their final conflict, and now, at the very last, when I feared I should lose her," a smile played across his lips, "she has taken a fatal step and two souls will be one."

He stopped suddenly, he had reached the garden gate of the cottage where he lived, the cottage, which for half a century (owing to a hideous crime committed within its walls) had been shunned as haunted. He had made himself the talk of half the county when, nearly three years ago, he had arrived and settled there with his Indian servant, a talk that had lowered to whispers of distrust as his answer to the clergyman's enquiries whether he was not afraid of having to give, as others had been forced to do, an account of the ghost circulating in the neighbourhood. "Ah no," he had replied in his slow prolonged accents, "I know the man well. I am stronger than he is; he is without knowledge." And whilst some held that he was mad and that the Indian was his keeper, the majority remained convinced that he was in league with the powers of darkness, and then to no good purposes; and so his acquaintance with the surrounding gentry ceased, and the country people would cross themselves as they hurried past him as if he were the fiend in person. All these outside affairs, however, passed him by as unheeded as the clouds of smoke from his cigarettes, and he continued to dream his dreams as he wandered in the woods or sat from morning till eve in his study. Into this room he now brought Winifred Owens, and, lifting some manuscripts from a chair, bade her be seated.

"Well now," he said, "you wanted me to do something for you, what was it?"

She raised her eyes and looked into his face. The nervous haste and excitement seemed to have passed from her to him. "Wait a moment," she cried, clasping her hands tightly over her eyes, "I am trying to think—what would be best for him."

Eugene Caruthers grasped the arms of his chair with his thin hands, on his hollow cheeks a spot of red burned, and into his eyes, from behind their darkness, flashed and flickered the hellish light that glows in the eyes of birds of prey when fearful of losing their victim. Rapidly he rose and with set pauses and murmured words, words which seemed to vibrate through his whole being, flinging out his delicately shaped hands and drawing the shape of a reversed pentagram in the air. Then, after waiting a few seconds, he flung himself into a chair paling and breathing as if exhausted. "What if I lost them after all," he cried to himself, "she has a weapon more powerful than mine if she knows how to use it." Flinging the black hair back from his forehead he cried again. "She shall look into my crystal instead of into her own heart, she shall look into the heart of Hell," and taking a large crystal from its stand he crossed the room, stood behind her chair and laying his hands over hers, drew them from her eyes and held the crystal before her.

"You are trying to look into your future. You will see it more easily in this and tell me what you see," he cried. "I will hold this to your forehead, it will help your view—tell me what you see now."

"I see his face," she said.

"Ah," murmured Caruthers, "he answers to this sign, already, does he? Good! then he shall help us against her and his own soul.

"Now what do you see?" he repeated in a voice that shook with excitement.

"I cannot see," said she. "There is a mist like tears, only I thought I could not cry."

"Fire dries tears," said Caruthers with an evil smile.

"Fire," she repeated. "Yes, yes, it is smoke, it is clearing away, yes there are flames—ah there is a dark figure with a mirror—she holds out her hand, it burns me, I cannot let it go, I cannot let it go! and she holds out her glass and in it is his face, I am looking in his eyes! Ah God! they too burn, they are like two bright spearheads thrust into my heart—I cannot draw mine from them, the ground is searing, the air is full of flames, I am breathing fire, not air——"

"Yes," said the young man, "I too felt this once. The figure is Memory with her glass and that is the face of the man you love and you could not forget it if you could, you would not if you could—and this is your life——"

"I would not if I could, no! and *this* is my life," and with an awful cry, the woman sprung up and snatched a lettered oriental dagger from a table nearby. "Oh, do as I asked! take away my soul and save me from this torture, if only for a moment, for an instant!"

He placed his hand on the dagger and drew it from her. "You chose this of your own——"

"Be quick," she cried stopping his words. "Oh, what can I say, what can I give you that will make you?"

"You need not trouble about that," he replied, "I shall be paid with the harvest of seven years, for I cannot do this thing for a moment—it must be seven years—do you agree?"

"Yes, yes," she gasped, "but if you have any pity be quick, I am in torture!"

"And you choose this of your own free will?"

"Yes," she replied, "be quick."

Eugene Caruthers smiled a smile of triumph as he laid her gently down on a couch by the window.

"Give me the dagger," she said.

He placed it in her hands and leaning forward he plucked one of the tall scarlet poppies that grew as high as the window sill, crushing it in his hand as he passed it over her burning brow, repeating as he did so words the meaning of which he himself did not wholly know, but whose vibrations shook his frame with so much force that he laid his hand on the couch for support. Her lips half parted in the beginnings of an awful cry of anguish—it died away in a sigh of content as sweet as that of a tired traveller who lies down to rest. For an instant, a convulsive effort shook her body—it ended in the peaceful heartbeats of a dreamless sleep.

Caruthers sunk into a chair and closed his eyes as if exhausted. The stillness in the room was intense. The summer sun shone on the trees and flowers that grew beyond the shadow of the house, the gnats hung motionless in the heavy air, the bees flew languidly from honeysuckle to foxglove, from foxglove to speedwell, speechlessly humming a drowsy song. The vine was thick around one side of the window and at the other a red rose grew and shed its petals soundlessly on the sill below, the large scarlet and white poppies stood like sentinels at the gateway of sleep. Inside Eugene Caruthers leaned back in his chair and stretched, he too was resting but every now and then he passed his hand across his brows and through the black hair that made the extreme paleness of his face appear yet more ghostly, and his eyes, lit no longer by the evil light of conflict, rested as if soothed upon the face of the sleeping woman. The silence grew and deepened.

Suddenly he roused himself and started up. "I must waste no more time," he cried, "I must guide her dreams." Yet he lingered looking at her; and bent forward and plucked several of the crimson roses and laid them over her heart. He unfastened the purple pansies that her lover had gathered that morning from her dress and wove them with white poppies around her brows. "They are but symbols," he said, "she shall both remember and forget."

And then he stood back and looked at her as a painter might look at a beautiful picture that he has just completed. She lay on the patchwork couch by the open window her head turned slightly to him, her face was still pale but a little colour was beginning to creep into her cheeks, the lines of anguish round her mouth had smoothed themselves into a smile, her eyes had found rest from their sorrow under the thick white lids. Her red gold hair lay all dishevelled round her brows and ivory throat as the red coloured leaves might lie when the storm is past, swept round the contours of some fallen idol, dark save where here and there the light from the swinging lamp above her caught and turned the red to gold, dying away again among the purple petals of the pansies. The stain from the scarlet poppy was still upon her forehead, one of its errant petals lay against her lips and through the roses that Eugene Caruthers had heaped about her hands gleamed her white fingers and through her fingers shone, with foul reflections creeping down it, the grey blade of the dagger.

"She was very fair even with a soul," he murmured, "how more than beautiful she will be without," and turning abruptly he left the room.

"Dabuji," he said, entering the hall and addressing the Indian manservant in his native language, "fetch me one of the hens and kill it."

"Sahib, there are none left," replied the man, "the last is dead."

Caruthers thrust his hands through his pockets with an air of impatient annoyance and stepped out across the garden into the wood. A dove was cooing in the distance to its mate, it stopped and listened for the answering note but it never came, and Eugene Caruthers hurried back to the cottage and threw the dead bird to his servant.

"Bring it in the little Egyptian bowl, and quickly," he said.

He paced up and down the hall while he waited, then, taking the bowl from the Indian, he entered the study and, dipping his fingers in the dove's blood, drew a line enclosing the

45

space where he stood by the sleeping woman, and, lighting a little brazier, he walked round it with set paces speaking in rhythmical tones in a language that was itself the ghost of a dead time an incantation. The smoke from the brazier began to thicken the air with mist and strange subtle fragrances till gradually all the objects without the blood-traced boundary line became obscure, and only the space in which he and the woman were remained daylit. But as the vapour rolled forward and touched this line it writhed, shuddered and separated itself into forms at first shadowy and undefined, but which grew quickly in substance and horror until they became at least as apparently substantial as the man who had raised them. They stood silently around the space of light awaiting his bidding. "I command you by this," and he stretched out both his hands and drew a sign in the air above their bent heads, "that you tell her and show her what I am willing."

One by one the evil shapes—some so hideous that they sent a thrill of horror even through Caruthers—bent above the couch and whispered to the sleeping woman the message of their master, while Caruthers stood with his brows drawn into one black line straight across his forehead and his bloodless hands clenched so fast with the culmination of his purpose that the bones and sinews stood out in strong white relief against the shadows they cast, guiding and restraining by his will the evil powers that he had raised. Gradually the colour rose in the woman's face as she turned uneasily and a little laugh and a few murmured words broke the silence, and one by one, their evil services rendered, the messengers of darkness faded back into the gloom and smoke. Eugene Caruthers extinguished the fire in the brazier, the vapour became thinner and thinner and at last faded away entirely. Then he bent forward and, passing his hand over Winifred Owen's brow, bid her wake.

With a start she sat up and looked around her, "Where am I?" she began and then broke off with a little laugh, "Oh Mr Caruthers you must forgive my—ah——" as the dagger round which she had suddenly closed her fingers left a red stain on their whiteness.

"Oh, I remember," she exclaimed, "I wanted to kill myself, didn't I? I recollect I wanted to kill myself because this man I loved threw me over for another woman! Oh, what a fool I was! I will do better than that now." The scarlet lips parted in a laugh that rang through the air, a laugh at the cadences of which the elemental shapes with which to Caruthers' beckons the room was crowded took clearer form and catching the echo passed it down to Hell. "Ah" she cried, springing up, "this is glorious! He shall come back again, he shall suffer as he made me suffer. I feel so strong," clutching her white hands, "I feel as if I had some new power."

"And so you have," he said, "see!" and he pointed to a full-length mirror at the end of the room. It reflected the same woman who had entered the room an hour before, then with wild eyes, white lips and quivering frame. Now the eyes gleamed with a light that held and fascinated. The lips, as scarlet as if the words that passed had burnt them, curved themselves into a mocking smile, on her cheeks between the whiteness of chin and brow glowed a rich deep colour like a flush of triumph and her hair shone around her like living flame. The light in her eyes and the smile around her lips deepened as she cried with a long drawn sigh of content, "I see my power—I am beautiful!"

"Yes," he replied, "you have no soul, for seven years you will remain thus. No tears of vain regret will dim those eyes, no sleepless nights of longing will make those cheeks pale, no darkened days of unendurable remembrance will let lines of anguish trouble those lips. Nor will lonely years of parting turn this gold to grey, and your idol shall be your slave. You shall have your revenge."

"Yes," she cried, "he will come back to me—I will have my revenge."

II

Her hour at last between Hell and Heaven!

THE summer sunlight shone bright even through London smoke into the room and fell full at Lady Weately's head as she stood in the window. Casually pulling to pieces the pansies in her hand, her eyes followed the petals as they fell like dark drops of blood upon the floor, but she was blind to the words of a man that fell like soft music on her ear, her hour of triumph had come.

"But you cared for me once," he pleaded, "I'd have staked my life that you would have been *that* to me and—and———"

"And you went away and married another woman and I married another man, well what was wrong?"

"I do not care *that* for her," he cried with a passionate gesture.

"And I never cared *that* for him," said she.

"It was only for money," Ledbury replied.

"It was only for money," she echoed mocking. "Really," she went on, "our motives are curiously alike, but after all what more desirable thing is there than money?"

"There is love," he cried madly.

She threw back her head and laughed aloud. Ledbury stepped forward with an oath. "You shall not laugh at me that like!" he exclaimed passionately, then his voice changed. "Oh, Winifred, Winifred, what has changed you so, have you no pity for me, do you not remember those old days when—when——"

"When you threw me over," she interjected. "Go on, this is amusing," she laughed again. It stung him through and through.

"Winifred," he cried, "you will drive me mad with your cruelty. Have you no heart or soul in you?"

"Ah no," she said clasping her hands with a pretty little gesture "that is the beauty of it, I have no soul, but," laughing still, "it does sound so funny to hear *you* talking about souls and yet do you know I once believed you had one and—I'll tell you the story, it will amuse you and change the current of your thoughts a little, for really I cannot stand tragedy for more than a minute or two. 'In the old days' as you will insist upon calling them, though strictly speaking, I believe it is not quite a year ago. Oh! Oh, I simply worshipped you, there was nothing I wouldn't have done for you, and now, well now I wouldn't—but I am wandering from my point, well that day you—but—bah! it makes me quite angry to think what a fool I was then and now—and now I must run and dress for Lady Hillier's, so adieu!" and looking back at him as she left the room: "You will dine with us tonight."

III

A couple of years later and a group of Winifred Weatly's intimate friends were discussing the fag end of the latest scandal in which she had figured as heroine. "I always said it would end so," remarked the hostess as she replaced the cup of a vivacious little brunette, who had just entered whilst full of the latest gossip, "everyone knows she married Sir Edward for his money, and of course Ledbury came in for treble as much, she chucked Weatly."

"Ledbury threw her over and married some other girl."

"Yes, and was a perfect brute to her, I believe. Anyway, she went back to her people and died conveniently."

"And shall you know her still, Mrs Chichester?" asked the youngest of the group.

"Yes, of course," replied the old lady. "Why, child, she's divorced and married, and—and in fact is quite a proper person again. You'll find that she is far too rich and fascinating to get badly cut."

So the years passed.

IV

Two blent hearts never astray,
Two souls no power may sever.

DOWN the stairs and through the heavily curtained doorway came the light sound of a woman's dress, and the man who was standing in the room looked up quickly as the curtain swayed aside and his wife entered. He went forward quickly.

"Well, you see I am back."

"Oh, Winifred, you are lovelier than ever, you are beautiful," he said, laying his hand on her arm.

"You didn't think so seven years ago," she said flinging it off lightly.

"*Seven* years ago," he replied, "is it possible, 'pon my soul you do not look a day older than you did then, no not as old, you've quite changed though in other ways, you used to be so serious then."

"I was an unmitigated fool—ah——ah!" a sudden cry of agony stopped the lecture. A ghastly whiteness grew upon her face. "Oh Hubert—Hubert!" she cried in anguish. "What have I done, my soul, what have I done!"

He tried in vain to soothe her, then laid her half-fainting on a couch and would have moved away to get assistance, but the lady clung wildly to him. "Oh, do not go," she cried, "for heaven's sake, do not leave me."

Hubert Ledbury sat by his wife holding her hands and trying to calm her, till even he got a little alarmed, and, calling a servant whom he heard passing, he sent for a physician. "Wini," he said, "you are looking awfully bad, you had better go to bed and we'll have a doctor in."

But the doctor, when he arrived, appeared about as helpless in the matter as Ledbury had been. All he could do was to say that Mrs Lebury seemed to have received a severe shock and that she was suffering from utter nervous prostration, and to order perfect rest and quiet.

So Winifred Ledbury lay the rest of the day in the darkened room, lay there and fought again the battle of seven years ago, while every minute that passed seemed as the fresh thrust of a knife into her being. When she rose again she was like the ghost of her former self.

At first Hubert Ledbury was sorry for his beautiful wife and tried his utmost to spare her from what he considered her nervous morbid fears, but when once she began, with wild eyes and trembling lips, to tell him what was troubling her he stopped her short. "Don't be so foolish, child," he said, "injure my what? Oh, ah, my soul, I think my dear, you would have to go a good long way before you could do that," Winifred shuddered. "I tell you what it is," he went on, "you've knocked yourself up with this everlasting ratcheting about, I shall take you down to the country. We'll go and stay at your old place."

"Oh Hubert," she gasped faintly, "don't, don't!"

"By heaven," he exclaimed, "but women are queer. Why, wasn't it only the other day that you wanted to know when the next train down was? Now be a sensible girl," and pulling out his watch, "let's go someplace this evening? I don't wonder you are in this state when you shut yourself from morning till night, and I shall telegraph to Hills to have the house ready."

So Fate in the form of Hubert Ledbury brought Winifred back to the scene of her former struggle. Once again she walked with him in the old ways where, seven years ago, they had lingered hand in hand, she with a happiness beyond all telling her heart, he with a few light lies upon his lips and a pleasant feeling of gratified vanity. Oh, yes, he cared for her certainly in a way, in a way that left it possible for him to care for Hubert Ledbury a hundred times more. And at her heart now was a burning fire, in his mind a vague feeling that he was getting a little bored.

Day by day, as he left her more and more alone, her steps wandered nearer and nearer to Caruthers' cottage, but each time she found whither they were leading she would turn and fly as if from some scene of horror. Day by day her face got thinner and paler and the youth and beauty that had fallen so suddenly from her seemed to grow further off, and day by day thus in vain she tried to keep him by her. Hubert Ledbury left her more and more alone and sought his amusement elsewhere. Winifred met him one day loitering down the lane with the Rector's pretty daughter, a girl that she had held in her arms as a baby. She caught her breath with a sudden gasp, it seemed the shadow of another torture, she stood after they had passed on as if irresolute which way to go. Twice she turned as if she would take the path through the wood to the cottage, where in one short minute all her trouble would be ended, then with a final effort pushed her way home.

"Hubert," she began that night at dinner, "I am getting tired of the country."

"And I," he interrupted, "was just going to tell you that I was getting sick of it, I leave tomorrow."

"Very well," she said, "I will be ready. What time?"

"Oh you know," he replied, "I—ah I think you'd be better down here wouldn't you, getting strong you know."

"You do not want me," she said, and the colour flushed all over her face as she rose.

Hubert Ledbury rose too. "Not want you and why not? I only thought," he patted her hand lightly, "that you didn't look so very fit just yet."

She flung his hand away from her. "Do not try this sort of thing over again!" she cried, "I learnt once how much it meant. You do not want me—you are getting tired of me——"

"I am getting tired of your nonsense," he said crossly.

For a few days Winfried Ledbury remained in the country, then she re-joined her husband and took up her old life again. She hated it now, hated still more the motive that prompted it—the feeling of unconquerable jealousy that had taken possession of her. "I cannot bear it," she would cry in her heart as day by day she saw Ledbury's eyes following with admiration another woman, the girl who had stepped into her place in the stakes of beauty, the girl between whom and herself was overheard such comparisons as these:

"Certainly pretty yes but cannot hold a candle to Mrs Ledbury, at least I mean as she was, the others will have some chance now; I never saw a woman go off so quickly as she has, she looks quite old now."

"Yes and Ledbury seems to think so too, he feels quite——"

She waited for no more, stung beyond all endurance, she left the crowded rooms and drove home. She determined that she would tell him all, that she would appeal to his pity, to his past love for her; and she flung herself into a chair and waited for his return, a consuming jealousy at her heart, and mixed with this was the revelation and remorse of her reawakened soul, her soul that seven years ago had been cast out of a body that was then a fit dwelling place for it, and now returned to this same body that, for seven years, had been the home of evil passions and had grown inwardly hideous with sin, a seething mass of pollution and corruption. And in this charnel house of dead beauty, imprisoned in this was her soul with its old purity, its old love for the man for whose sake it had been cast aside.

Winifred Ledbury realised it all, realised how she had lowered his soul, how she had helped and persuaded, yes, even guided him in the path of evil and quenched with light laughter and mockery the few faint flames of higher life, and this had been the result of one mad act that he had driven her to, with the return of her soul the old fight had recommenced, the old temptation had come back a hundredfold more strong, the old love deeper than ever, he was not now the man who had been her husband for four out of the seven years, he was her love of old, for whose sake all this had come upon her.

The light of dawn crept slowly through the room and met but did not mingle with the light of the lamp, even as the light of her soul met and strove with the fierce flame of passion, by and bye she rose and, pulling aside the curtain, looked out. There above the dark house and the gloomy street stretched the fair, pale dawn-blessed sky, the pearly grey slid into pearly opal, the opal into a sea of rose where the lilac clouds rippled like hope-flushed waves as if they would cross the grey and opal, and enter the wide expanse of blue beyond. For a minute she felt the message of peace and hope, her eyes looked into the heart of the new-born day, her lips repeating unconsciously a verse, the words of which had, since the day she read them first, woven themselves into mystic meaning round her life.

"Even here when Heaven holds breath
  and hears
The beating heart of Love's own breast,—
When round the secret of all spheres
All angels lay their wings to rest,—
How shall my soul stand rapt——"

Her voice faltered, the tears rushed into her eyes and falling on her knees by the window she wept painfully.

The sound of Ledbury opening the hall door roused her, and she sprung up, hastily drying her tears; she knew by this time how he hated "scenes", she tried with trembling hands to smooth her disordered hair; she drew the curtains again and turned the lamp a little lower and went forward to the door to stop him on his way upstairs.

"Hubert," she began nervously, "I have waited up for you,"

"Indeed," he replied, "I think you'd have been wiser if you hadn't. Late hours don't seem very good for you," he went on, looking with an air of critical disapproval at her. "You've quite lost your complexion and you're growing thin, and——"

"Old," she added.

He lifted his shoulders slightly. "Oh, you aren't so very old," he rejoined, "not nearly as old as I am and in fact as good looking as ever, I think." He threw back his head with its strong beautifully moulded features, and glanced at her with a mocking look in his eyes.

"Oh Hubert," she cried, "have some pity on me! Do you not see I am suffering for your sake, that every minute I live is a struggle against the blessed relief of Death or the relief of worse? Do you not know that day you parted with me in the wood that I tried to drown myself, and I could not because I felt that I might do you harm and yet this torture was so horrible that I—I parted with my soul that I might find rest in death. That was sin. I thought I could kill myself then, but when I woke soulless I no longer wished for death. I laughed at what I thought my folly; I felt a glorious lust of life and beauty and power and, stronger than all these, a thirst for revenge. Had I any pity for your wife? For you? For my husband? I have heaped sin after sin upon my conscience! and all these are light—light—compared with the thought that I have drawn you down with me. I seem to have made you the author of all my guilt by this one mad act, I feel as if I had built round you and me an environment of evil that will be too strong for us to fight against. Life after life we shall—Oh Hubert," she broke off, wildly clutching his hand and falling on her knees before him, "will you try and save yourself—if you have any pity or love left for me do this thing—do you not know it is only for your sake that I remained in this torture—that in a few short hours I could be as fair and young as ever and——"

"By heaven," cried the man, "I wish you would then. *I'd* be very glad—you were the loveliest woman I ever saw. Bah!" he exclaimed, throwing her hand roughly away from him. "You make me sick with your infernal hysterical nonsense, you'd better be careful or I'll have you shut up as a lunatic."

"And then perhaps you could marry again?" she said, crying and standing a few paces further. "I'm afraid that wouldn't be as easy to manage—however it's a good idea. I'll think over it."

Don't be such a fool," he said lightly and left the room.

She stood for a few moments as he had left her then turned to go. "I will go back to Hertsmere tomorrow," she said in parting.

In passing she glanced at a mirror by the door, was it a ghost that looked back at her from its smooth surface with hollow cheeks and sunken eyes, with lines of pain around the lips and brows, the ghost of the former self with youth and beauty fading, slipping from her? "No wonder he is tired of me," she cried. "I am beautiful no longer—and—and I myself taught him this creed!"

For weeks after she reached the country she lay exhausted. She wrote once to her husband telling him that she was ill, praying him to come to her. He replied after the lapse of a week, a few words undated from the Despard's house, beginning with some questions about money and ending with an admonishment "not to be a fool."

"Yes," she said slowly, "he has ceased to care for me. He is with her now. No—no, I will not bear it, I will go," and springing up, "to——"

"Mr Caruthers" announced the servant, flinging open the door, and Caruthers entered.

"Well," he said, holding out his hand.

"Yes! Yes!" she cried "take away my soul—give me back my youth, my beauty and him! Oh, Hubert! Hubert, my love, is there no power, no power will help me, will save us, I cannot—I will not——" and dashing madly past Caruthers she rushed out into the garden, down the road and through the wood, whither she knew not.

The ground was thick with withered fallen leaves, the stream had become a little river from the late rains, the river a foaming roaring torrent, the wooden bridge swayed and shivered as the waters swept round it, and a group of men on the opposite side raised their voices and shouted warning after warning as they saw with horror a woman flying as if for her life alight such certain death.

The warnings did not reach her ears, her hands covered them in an effort to shut out the low poisonous voice of Eugene Caruthers which seemed to follow and tempt her still.

One man from the group sprung forward, shaking off the restraining hands that should have held him back, heading not the voices that warned it was certain death, that he could not save her.

"She shall not die alone!" he cried, and as the bridge crashed beneath her weight, he reached her side as she sank in the water below, her head sank on her lover's breast and as their bodies were hurled along the raging flood their souls passed together into the land of fulfilment.

And Caruthers, watching from afar, shuddered and turned with a curse from the spot.

"I have lost them both!" he cried.

ASPIRATION

A CRAMOISIE PAVILION glowed like a giant fungus among the trees of the forest! Round it clustered other tents, green, blue, flame-colour, purple and vermillion, one or two larger, but none half so splendid, for the canvas walls of the cramoisie pavilion were overhung with silk, while the cords that bound it to earth—and indeed to bind it seemed necessary, so dream-glowing and fairy-woven did it appear—were of red silk twisted with gold. It was the pavilion of the Princess Hedonia— she who had come, worn out with the clangour and unrest of the court to seek new life in the green quiet of the wood—flooding this forest space with her glittering retinue. guardians, governesses, the court physician, the court-poet, ladies-in-waiting, knights and pages, dancers, lute-players, singers, the court jester, dwarfs, the head of these being her chief sandaller, serving maids, cup bearers, mirror bearers, slaves, and a multitude of others. The court physician, whose words at this crisis of the Princess' illness were of more account than those of the chancellor even, had smiled grimly when he had seen the cavalcade ready to set out, and, arrived at the forest, he had allowed them just six pastoral hours; at the sign of sundown ordering them back again far out of sight and hearing of the Princess. One sleep-seeking old governess, a simply shy maid-of-honour but lately come to the court and still sighing for a country home, and a serving maid, more simple still, he kept. The chief cook and his Scullions he sent packing and gave his tent into the hands of a red-checked country wench, whose chief qualification was her inability to produce any but country fare, and that of the plainest. These and a handful of grizzled knights, some archers to procure food, and a little page as messenger to the town, were all he kept out of the gay hundreds who passed in rivers under his stern eye. He stroked his pointed beard in debate as the jester reached him, and caused him to stand a minute, and then dismissed him summarily, for no other reason than the man's incapacity to keep his tongue from clacking even in that minute's space. The court poet he waved townwards with fierce gesture, while yet he was but in sight, and so too with the dancers, the lutists, the singers, he shooed them from him like a head shepherd with an unruly flock. The angry dwarfs had to scurry and trot to keep pace with the general stampede, and even the Princess laughed lightly, forgetting her languor and chagrin at the sight.

Nine tents instead of the hundred she had devised composed the encampment. Through the trees could be seen, smoothly clipped and groomed, the she-asses that were to supply the Royal Pavilion with milk, gleaming like clouds as they grazed in the meadows beyond the wood. Their manes were close cropped and their tail-tufts tassel-wise and dyed scarlet, and the pale horn of their hoofs was polished and inlaid with various metals.

The wood-folk, who peered, astonished into excitement or timorousness, from the trees and undergrowth, watched with curious eyes: the dryads regarded the dancing of the court dancers with scorn in their hearts. Even the most supple dancer in Asia seemed as a tyro in the art that was nature to them, and at the sound of the lutes, the satyrs half-raised their pipes to derisive lips. When the singers sang, and the little group of syrens that had swum up the creek and river to join the naiads, laughed softly, that whispered fugitive laughter made the sweeter music. But the gay colours of the dresses and the tents, and the glitter of armour and of gold and silver cups and platters and jewels, and the henna-stained hair and painted cheeks of the Human Folk attracted, even while the bustle and the commotion of their coming affrighted the wood-people. The great cornelian-red hound of the little princess came among them in amity. When the sun went down upon the rejected cavalcade on its homeward road and upon a meal laid on the greensward, so novel in its simplicity that, to the Princess, it tasted more delicious than any banquet she could remember, she strolled, with delicate blue-veined hand on the collar of the red hound, her maid by her side and the physician and a grey knight tree-hidden some few paces behind, into the mazes of the forest. The honey-gold moon rose, over dark branches and the nightingales sang; and the old physician, in consideration of having ruthlessly robbed her of her glittering retinue, suffered her caprice for an hour longer than he was willing. And the young faun who had first espied her coming drew nearer and nearer in the silence of her listening, and the shadow of the trees, and looked right into the pale grey eyes that were set between gilded brows and painted cheeks, and loved the Princess Hedonia! All that night, after the red pavilion had folded her in, he watched crouched beside the great hound at the uncurtained entrance, and heard her sigh in her sleep, and turn restlessly; and for the first time in his life disquietude mingled with joy in his heart and oppressed him.

A whole moon the Princess Hedonia dwelt in the forest, sighing less, as the days slipped by, for the life she had left in the white walled city across the creek of mirroring sea. She had wept and upbraided and sulked all for no purpose; the court physician had stood grimly looking on, recommending calmness or cheerfulness, as the case might be, his counsel flavoured with decoctions of lunary and alkanst, although his sovereign remedy seemed to be bathing in the sunlight or even the little blue rivulet that ran sea-wards past the outskirts of the forest. But by and by the Princess' ennui had given place to interest in her surroundings. It was in one of these woods that she first perceived the faun. She often wished to see such a creature, and had once offered a prodigious reward for taking one. She desired to add it to her retinue and would have had its shaggy fleece cut and combed and curled, and its hoofs, gilt and spanciled with silver chains, so that it might not flee again to the forest, But, although the reward was great, the peasants and shepherds had failed to snare one of these timid creatures who withdraw themselves from human view at will, nor indeed even in those days could all people see them. But here was a faun to her hand! He crouched his chin upon his palms, gazing at her with great dark eyes eloquent of trust. The little Princess, who desired all eyes turned on her with admiration, felt curiously abashed beneath the gaze of the simple woodhouse. Not so the faun! He greeted her cognition by stretching out both hands with the frank gesture of a child. The Princess, with a glance at her maid-of-honour, who was sighing over her lace pillow with its maze of bright coloured bobbins, put a hand in one of his and went with him into the forest, her red hound following. It was after this that she began to grow light-hearted and threw off her langours and sought the sunlit spaces bare-browed, and kilted up her long, flowing gown and then discarded it altogether, sending her serving-maid a-fairing to bring her and her lady-in-waiting a gown, apiece of the guise worn by the peasant wenches of that country-side. Clad thus she masqueraded bare-footed in the forest, wearing the garlands of flowers and leaves that the faun twined for her. By the end of the second week, when the woods were growing rich with Autumn stains and the leaves glowing against the sun like gold and sard and fire-opals with here and there in the bramble bushes a leaf of ruby tincture, some of the Season's colour had come upon her face, her cheeks grew bright as the spindle fruits, her hands and feet brown as the bracken fronds, and her lips like the scarlet berries of the wild rose. The faun taught her wood-dances and to run fleetly and jump the streams and the fallen trees. She ate of the wood-berries and of the homely fare, rye-bread, oat-cake, curd-cheeses and cream with a hearty hunger that made the old physician smile. She lived like the faun, in the joyful hour that is, and thought but little of the city across the sea. As for the faun he did not think at all beyond the delight of their fair friendship. The bright hours passed for him but as steps in a dance of joy. It seemed a world of gold and azure beauty and the mists as the smoke of Summer's pyre—the fragrance of the earth itself—more powerful and pervading in Autumn than at any other season. The days were as hot as Summer's days and only the faintest cold breath came at early morn and at eve. The Princess, with high-kilted kirtle, would run hand-in-hand with the faun through the forest, seeking the blue haze that eluded even their swiftest running.

"We will be King and Queen of the Blue Land!" said the little Princess, laughing.

"It is there, through that hornbean arch," said the faun. But when they gained the arch and passed through it, their world was still gorgeous with the red and gold of Autumn and the enchanted land still afar! And they would laugh like two children well content and but playing with a hardly desired faery-land. Then suddenly one day as they were talking home-ward to the pavilion, they met the physician who looked curiously at the Princess and said:

"Your sire, the King, has sent a messenger to bid you return tomorrow."

The Princess stamped upon the ground till the twigs snapped under her bare brown feet.

"I do not wish to return." she said.

"The Messenger is Prince Mondain," continued the physician and the faun saw a flame of colour leap into her face, and she dropped his hand and questioned:

"Where is he?" and hung her head like an abashed child, and then said:

"How sun-burned I am. Pray, kind physician, tell me of what herb will quickest wash this uncomely brownness off me," and looking disdainfully at her hands she drew up her sleeves and showed him the sharp contrast of cloud-white and sun-burned skin. But he only smiled his grim smile and she reddened yet more and said pleadingly: "Go and keep him in converse for a space till I gain my pavilion and put on a more worthy apparel than the garb of a shepherd-maid." And the physician went to do her wish.

A breath colder than the first breath of Winter blew in the faun's heart and shook the flame of it this way and that. He touched her hand, but she cast him off absently and went without a glance at him in the direction of the pavilion. He saw her eyes shining and her cheeks glowing and her lips smiling, and he knew that this was for something beyond him and the forest. He watched her going swiftly from him till she passed into the Blue Land that they together had not found. And the first tears he had shed fell unheeded down his brown cheeks.

The next day the forest was all astir and aglitter again—for the King had sent an escort yet larger than the one with which the Princess had arrived. The pavilion was taken down and while this was being done, the Princess wandered with the Prince in the wood. She no longer went bare-foot. The chief dwarf had sandalled her, sighing, after bathing her feet in fennel water; and gold and purple and jewels shone upon the fallen leaves, and purple and gold and rose-embroidery swept them as she passed, and the Prince in shining argent and scarlet drew out his sword and cut the brambles from her path. Her hair was no longer free and crowned with forest flowers, but was braided elaborately and bound with a heavy chaplet of gold and precious stones, and her gilded eyelashes fell upon cheeks the brownness of which was hidden by white and red unguents. The faun dropped the wreath of

Traveller's Joy he had woven for her and stood aside in the bushes. She did not see him even as she passed . . . From far off he watched the preparations for the start, and saw the stranger lift the Princess on to a great chestnut horse and the cavalcade set out. With heart dumb with incredulous grief he followed it in the lingering hope of some regard from her. As the white road came in sight, he grew desperate and ran through the horsemen to her side and, grasping her floating gown, besought her not to leave him. And the Princess, who but a few hours back had gone hand-in-hand with him, looked at him in anger and bade him be gone. None of all the gay troup saw him, but only she. And the more she upbraided him, the more he clung to her crying upon her, till the sound of this wailing, which had in it so much of human grief, became audible to those around and one or two of the young knights, desirous of adventure, turned in their saddles and said:

"Is not there a cry of distress in the brake afar-off?"

But Princess Hedonia said:

"'Tis but a snared rabbit. It will cry louder yet," and she lifted her whip and struck the faun with all her might across his up-turned face, and therewith he ceased his wailing, but his tears fell silently upon the bright silk of her gown, and she struck with her sharp-spurred heel hard against his arm till the blood flowed down upon the golden-embroidered hem, and when she got to the road she put her horse to the gallop and the faun ran with till his breath failed, and he dropped from her side on the sward by the roadway and flung himself down, hiding his eyes from the sight and ears from the sound of her going. He lay there sobbing till sleep hushed him and darkness drew round him, and then, after a space, he awoke and wandered through the night far from the forest where he and the Princess had danced together. He went seawards and saw it gleam beneath him, and he climbed a little rock and watched, broken-hearted, the lights lit in greeting for Princess Hedonia.

At dawn he hid in a near coppice, and night after night he would come to the rock and watch from the lights in the city beyond the creek and their broken images upon the waters. And this he did for many nights and went weeping at dawn. But one night he turned and looked seaward and saw the reflections of the Stars gleaming there, and looked from them to the sky, and saw them flash and shine in unshaken radiance far beyond the power of the waves. Night after night as his vigil drew to a close he looked at the city of stars for comfort, and gradually he gazed less and less at the lights in the city on the sea and more and more at the stars, and, as he gazed, rapt with voiceless aspiration, luminous wings grew, dim at first, but brightening to radiance. The night came when he did not look at all on the city below him! And this was the night on which it was all illuminated from turret to lagoon in honour of the marriage of the Princess Hedonia!

Some peasants passing by this rock next morning found the dead body of a young faun lying at the foot of it, and remembering the Princess' caprice, and hoping for a goodly largesse, took it up and bore it to her. But she gazed at it in white horror and, flinging gold to them, bade them bury the body where they had found it. This was but a fleeting mood that momentarily shocked her, and after, as the passing years stole the smoothness from her skin and the brightness from her hair and she became insistent of admiration, she would tell her lovers, wantonly and with vain perversions, the story of the faun:

"So great was his love for me that he cast himself from this rock on my bridal night", she, who knew naught of stars or wings, would say, sitting on a grave as shallow and empty as her own heart, for the peasants, eager to join in

the carnival, cast the faun's body into the sea,
and at leisure, on the morrow, raised a false
grave beneath the rock.

Did the radiant wings bear him to the stars?
    Far beyond!

THE CHRISTMAS CRIB

THE CHURCH stood in a clearing of the great forest. None knew if the house of God had been there first as some hermit's place of rest, and the village had grown round it, or if the village had grown first, and the church had been sent to its inhabitants for their need; but be that as it may there the church stood, beautiful and calm, all white and silver in the pure air. Beautiful inside too with the intangible virtue of true devotion and peace, and with the more visible devotion of art in zealously carved stone and in richly coloured glass. It was a place of joy and of deep peace. Fragrant airs from the pines were wafted into it from outside, and the sweetness of incense went floating out from it into the forest.

The old priest, Father Theophilus, served there in love and joy. To him all the villagers were as his sons and daughters, but even as a mother will seem more tender to the babe in her arms, so was his heart towards the children of his flock. He would tell them glad and beautiful things of their true home, and fair things too of their transitory earthly one, and he would play and laugh with them at their games, and show them the way to conquer their difficulties. He taught them to read and write, as there was no school-master in the village. They were dear to his heart. He himself was nearly as poor as the villagers, far poorer than one or two of the richer farmers, and worked in his garden and the field, and sowed and reaped like them, harder even, because he so loved flowers that he spent most of his leisure time in his garden, where were the flower-borders that folded in the great white and gold lilies and the red and white roses which decked the altar, and towered above the lowlier flowers that grew at their feet. Heartsease white and purple, gold and brown; clove pink, crimson, white and streaked columbines, pale pink and purple and shadowy white, and in which the little children loved to find the doves—and honey flowers white and golden for the bees. Many other delectable flowers made a fragrant and coloured loveliness through Spring, Summer and Autumn, till Winter wrapped the bare stems and withered leaves in whiteness, and the Earth held close to her warm heart the gold and the jewels and incense of the season.

Many little parables did the good father make for the children from his flowers and bees, for of these last he kept many hives, and from them his housekeeper would take the honey that they yielded to the neighbouring market, where the townspeople would flock to buy it as the sweetest, richest, most golden honey of all the country round. With this money Father Theophilus would buy small comforts for his old, poor and sick, gifts for his youths and maids who wedded, or went out to seek their fortune in the great world, and toys and sweets for the children. For two years he had been saving from this little flower harvest to buy a crib for the church at Christmas, and he pictured the delight of the children when they should see so fair and wonder-wakening a sight for the first time. He liked to think how through the joyous labours of these small brothers of men such things came. And he would gather the children round the hives in Winter and let them feed the bees with the bee-food the housekeeper made to supply the place of the honey taken from them. And when there were no flowers left in the garden to tell them stories about, he would show them the beautiful flowers of the snow crystals, and talk to them of the brave holly, and tell them the names and virtues of the steadfast planets and the shining flashing stars, and of the great star that lead the shepherds and the kings through the blue night to the cattle-shed at Bethlehem.

This year of which I tell had worn round in beauty to the Eve of Christ. The church was decorated with garlands and wreaths, green shone clear against, or in shadowy places, melted into the white or grey of the walls and pillars. Red and black and white berries gleamed here and there against the green. On the Altar were the white flowers that Father Theophilus grew each year with such care for the Feast of Love. Beside them shone the candles like little golden stars. Outside was the great forest which the peasants dreaded after the dusk had filled it, for there lived the wood-people, and the wood-cutters or any wayfarers passing through it would cross themselves and hurry on without looking round if they heard a sound in the under-growth through which the paths had been cut. Outside too was the snow which levelled all the graves and drew a lovely veil over those symbols of newly made grief, for which dim mortal eyes still wept. The roof and the little stone saints that guarded the door were cloaked in its softness too, and the warmth and colour of the glowing eastern window fell across its whiteness like the sound of praise upon the silence of peace. All around, save where the roads branched to the village, the graveyard melted into the wood, only a few holly and yew bushes marking where the graves ceased. Beyond were the great forest trees, some bare in their deep Winter sleep, and some still wrapt in their dark enduring leaves, from which the snow, overweighing some large bough, would slip with a dull thud to the ground, and the branch would spring up again, green from its white burden.

The path to the great door which stood wide open, golden in the greeting, was swept clean. Little feet had just ceased clattering up it, and all the children of the village stood in the broad side-aisle round where, in a wide niche, the Priest had set up the christmas crib. There was the little Christ Child laid in the straw of the manger, stretching out his hands to the cold world. And there was the Blessed Mary, his mother, kneeling in adoration by him, her blue cloak falling in soft folds over her rose-red dress on to the yellow straw, and on the other side knelt St. Joseph in his rough brown coat and under-coat of purple. There too were the Shepherds clad in the wool of their flocks, and there, gorgeous in scarlet and purple, crimson and green, silver and gold knelt the three kings, the young, dreaming Caspar, the old wise Melchior, and in the years between them the dark, ardent troubled King Balthazar. Their jewelled crowns were on the ground, and their offerings of gold and frankincense and myrrh in their hands, and behind them all were the patient toilers for man, the ox and the ass. And because the artist who had carved these fair little images and felt the goodness that emanated from Father Theophilus, and because he too laboured for the same master, and because the lovely mystery of Christmas-tide had filled his heart with devotion, he had added as a gift to the group two little kneeling Angels, their hands and wings folded, their faces uplifted in song. The priest had made a small wattle fence and wooden manger, and hung a great lanthorn high up out of sight so that the light poured down upon the figures as the rays from the guiding star. All the rest of the church except the great altar he had left in dim, or dark shadow so that the light from the crib should shine out more radiantly into the darkness. There in the wide aisle stood the children gazing almost in silence. Just now and then a long-drawn breath or whispered exclamation of admiration and wonder, or the sound of their wooden shoes as some drew back and others pressed forward.

Dearly was good Father Theophilus rewarded for his toil when he saw how, more deeply than words could reach, the beauty of the pictured story, told by these coloured bright little images, had sunk into the childish hearts. And he let them, after the first silence of delight and wonder, whisper amongst themselves.

"See the little Christ Child is stretching out His hands to us." "And that his mother is kneeling by him." "And look! look! the kings have given him their great gold crowns!"

And then, when all had looked their fill, he made them sing again the "Gloria in Excelsis" and a simple carol, one of such as were written for simple folk in those days, and he told them again in a few words that most lovely story of the first Christmas in Bethlehem. And as the children left the church singing again of glory to God and peace among men, the old priest stood at the open door, and listened to their voices as they went their homeward ways, some to the cottages near around, and some, all close together, the little ones holding the bigger ones' hands for fear of the wood-folk, through the dark forest paths. "Gloria in Excelsis" came floating to him from between the dark trees, where the lanterns flickered like ruddy will o' whispers, he listened till they broke into a simple carol they had sung around the crib.

Smiling Father Theophilus went back into the empty silent church and knelt by the glowing Altar, praying long for the beauty of Christ's Brotherhood to grow in these children's hearts and in the hearts of all, and in his own, thanking God too in humility that he had been led to follow the star that had brought him thus far on his path. And after so praying he remained kneeling in praise and adoration for a space, filled with love and peace and joy.

He was roused at last by a timid pattering of little hoofs on the stones of the side-aisle. Rising from his knees he went down the Altar steps through the dark chancel to where the crib glowed like a coloured star. There gazing at it—even as the other children had gazed—his small brown hands clasped in delight and wonder—stood a little wood-child!

The priest, who had expected but a straying goat, was aghast! and when the small creature began clapping its hands and singing in a wild sweet voice the echo of the children's Gloria, and its little goat's feet moved swiftly in a joyous rhythmic dance, the traditions of long years again the wood people filled his mind and darkened heart and bade half unconsciously move menacingly towards the satyr-child to drive him from the holy place.

Timid by reasons of long years of man's injustice the little creature threw one startled glance at the Priest, and with a wild shriek of terror fled to the door, its hard hoofs clattering over the graven stones.

At the sound of those little frightened flying feet that seemed to Father Theophilus to be beating on the hardness of his heart the old ill-will and darkness of the past fell from him, and snatching the lantern from the church porch the good father ran out into the night after the woodling crying "My Child, my Child, return." It was plainly to be seen, a small swift figure jumping the graves and scattering showers of snow from its flying hoofs. Into the darkness of the forest it plunged, and after it ran the priest who could still hear the shrill voice of mingled fear and anger that seemed more fierce, and disappointment that seemed more bitter, than in the crying of a human child.

Tears of pity and penitence streamed down the priest's face as he ran, those sorrowful cries piercing his heart like arrows from out of the darkness. Deeper and deeper into the forest the faun fled and the priest followed. Here and there, where there was a clearing and the moonlight fell upon the snow, he could see a small dark figure racing from him into the kinder darkness. At one larger clearing he nearly gained its side, but as it saw him following it screamed again its wild poignant cry, and fled with greater speed behind a great clump of holly-trees; the priest too followed and found himself suddenly in a place of Light!

There knelt the little wood-child, and there the Christ Child smiled and stretched out hands of love and welcome to him. Lovely, lovely was the vision glowing against the darkness of the forest depths. A golden radiance greater than the radiance of the sun shone round the head of the Holy Child, and more soft and tender than mellow moonlight was the light round the head of the Blessed Mother, and there too were St. Joseph and the shepherds and kings and the ox and the ass, and in the place of the two little angels in Father Theophilus' poor painted wooden crib were many great winged angels coming and going about the place of birth. The colours of skies and clouds and stars, the colour of the seas and of tranquil waters, the colours of flowers and leaves, and of precious stones, and the colours of fire seemed to shine upon their wings and illuminate all the space. The air seemed full of music, golden and silver, and charged with mists of light, more melodious than any he could have dreamed, and fragrance beyond any sweetness of earthly flowers or incense was all about.

With a great cry the priest fell upon his knees, but when the little satyr-child heard this cry and looking round saw the old man kneeling in the shadow far from the warmth and light, his childish heart, being full of Love and goodwill, bade him trot across the snow to him. Hand in hand with a great signing Angel came the wood-child and held out a small brown hand to Father Theophilus so with the angel guiding him on the other side the old man came close unto the mystery . . . There knelt the priest between heaven and earth, wrapt with the wonder, while the world passed from him for a space, and he knew no more of it until he awoke from his ecstasy and found that he was kneeling in the snow far in the heart of the forest. Then did he know that he had seen a vision of the divine love, that goes so much deeper than the love of man, caring tenderly for even the least of its creatures, and slowly, filled with peace, and the joys of this vision, Father Theophilus rose and went his homeward way, hearing still from out of the darkness of the trees until the distance drowned it, a childish honey-sweet voice singing joyfully of glory to God and peace and goodwill among men.

Long years after when good Father Theophilus had gone to rest in heaven, the children's children's children of those who had stood round the little crib that far off Christmas-tide wondered as they passed by the grave of the good priest's cast-off body, who put upon it the offerings of the first and rarest wood-flowers of Spring, the loveliest of wild roses of Summer, the most purple and golden berries and leaves in Autumn, and in Winter holly that was more splendid in leaf and berry than any that they could find.

And then the young priest—to whom had been handed down from priest to priest a little book, all fair with the gold and black and red of letters, and glow of little bright jewel-like pictures with golden upon them, wrought by Father Theophilus in his leisure hours—would gather the children together and tell them the story of the old Priest and his little brother the wood-child that Christmas Eve such long years ago . . .

For in this book was told the story of the vision, told in fair script and colour, and there on each page, playing sometimes with the little Angels on a flowery mound, or sitting in the quaint twistings of some decorating branch or flowering pattern of holly or vine, or peeping, shy-eyed, from behind a lily stem was the little wood-child. And the young priest would tell them how the grave of Father Theophilus, dug at eve, and left empty to the night, was found lined soft with dew-fresh flowers at dawn, starry with many-coloured wind-flowers, blue with hyacinths, golden with daffodils and Roses and silver with Amaryllis and Lilies, till from the loveliness of these stories the children lost all fear of the wood-people and would stop and sing the gloria and the old carol at the Holly bush that still marked the place where Father Theophilus knelt that Christmas Eve, long and long ago, in brotherhood with heaven and with earth.

WINTER

WE are too apt to think of Winter as a colourless, cold season, a time of discomforted waiting, to be endured with what cheerfulness we can muster, and we draw curtains close, shutting out the glory of her night skies, and blinded by discontent hasten past the glowing of her wet fields; although indeed the gathering of families and friends round our hearths is part of her teaching; for is chiefly of Winter and in Winter that there comes and remains throughout our earth-life, the wonder and joy of mystery, the awakening to the real, though seeming-far, voice of our inmost nature.

To the Western child it comes as a mystery of love and joy at Christmas, the great hearth-light of the world. To this light the flower of the imagination opens in the child's still eager mind, receiving the sun and the breath of a world not yet forgotten.

In former days the great revelation of Christmas drew forth a desire and response towards those super-material worlds on which is shed light: Mystery plays were acted and tales told, not only of angelic beings, but also of a multitude of lesser elemental creatures, elves, gnomes, ouphens or faries, and told not merely to while away the tedium of the long evenings but because the call of Winter had evoked a deeper consciousness and with the awakening of this consciousness, a sympathy with these beings: for if a few could actually see, most could cognise in some degree, the existence of inhabitants of another plane of being, a plane which is in reality, shared by man.

Now that the reign of a restricted science is passing and scientific intellects are being put more frequently freer uses, many minds are becoming anxious to explore recovered worlds, and we listen to old tales with a new interest and understanding which will lead us far on the road to freedom.

By thus awakening from ignorance of or hostility to these elemental brothers, we give forth a welcome and allow the virtue of the light to stream in upon us and allay the fear with which man in the dark ages used to regard these children of Nature, and assuage the distrust with which these children have learned to regard man—that mutual aversion which has so narrowed man's freedom. I think that if one so awakened were to go into the silent wintry fields and woods, he might be recognised as a brother by these shy creatures which now shun him, and might commune with Nature through her estranged children, as he could at no other season of the year.

Winter receives us as novices, seeking initiation, and, in return for a willing abandonment of less spiritual desires, rewards us with an insight into her mysteries: this it appears to me is why she is a time of greater magic than even manifesting Spring.

As Spring calls joyfully to the emotions, so Winter calls to the life that transcends emotion, and by lowering with her mighty elements our physical vitality, withdraws us somewhat from the dominion of the senses and brings us to a knowledge of our super-physical powers. This the other seasons with all their abounding appeal of colour, sound, fragrance, and heat rarely achieve.

She is indeed the Mother of Faith; of Faith, so steadfast that the light of Fulfilment may be seen about her.

Three other seasons go garlanded, chapleted, or crowned—she aureoled! It is a significant fact that it is in the depths of Winter and under the seemingly stern planet, Saturn (called by ignorance, "the great malefic") that the saviours of the world are born. I believe that the shining hosts seen in an exalted moment by the simple shepherds are still with us, waiting only for the clearing of the dust of the material from our eyes to be our heralds and guides.

And with this celestial host a company of lesser beings, those fairies of wisdomful children's' tales, those joyful guardians of tree and flower . . . whose work is the wide-spreading of beauty, the purity of which, we, their brothers, with the confusion and illusions of human consciousness, fail so lamentably to understand.

One can indeed live on this lovely earth a magical life that is lovelier than the life of the old magic tales; we can each Spring renew our youth as a child and young garlanded lover, each Summer we may follow, as a chapleted knight, our high adventure, each Autumn become a crowned and kingly harvester, but for Winter we must abandon garland and chaplet and crown, and stripping ourselves of green and crimson and gold, go naked into the wilderness, as pilgrim-neophytes seeking the unknown path.

For those who so dare, rather one should say, who so love, her darkness, her coldness, her storms, are guides and ministers.

To the man willing, as many are now becoming willing, to turn from the fret and false ideals of modern life, and to live more harmoniously with Nature, Winter may become recognisable as a time of pause, and rest, peace and contemplation; a time of shorter physical labour, of longer slumber, and in sleep a longer and conscious freeing of the Souls: a time of sacred fast from the feasting of the senses; the Vigil of the Festival of Immortal Spring!

SELECTED VERSE

DE PROFUNDIS
(TO A BEAUTIFUL VOICE)

OUT of the deeps, O voice, out of the
    deeps
You call the long unwept; and my heart weeps.

You call the long unprayed; and my heart
    prays,
And the long years only as short days.

O marvellous voice, cease singing, cease!
    O cease!
Lest my will, overcome at last—release

My Conqueror Captive. Lest I run to greet
The heart I have forbidden mine to meet.

AN OLD IRON CROSS WROUGHT WITH LILIES AND A ROSE

ALL who look upon this thing
See Love conquer suffering!
All who weep and all who pray
See the hard cross fade away.
—See the dawning of the Day.
(O come look upon this thing.)

Peace of lilies where those Hands
Stretched with healing o'er all lands.
Lilied Peace above that Head.
And where Holy Blood was shed
Haloed by the rose's red.
(Break our hearts, O tender Hands.)

This white Peace and this red Joy
Grief is powerless to destroy.
And the gold Heart of the Rose!
—Known alone of him who knows

This the Cross whereon it glows!
(Give us Peace and give us Joy.)

Long dead Artist, what Divine
Sorrow made you give this sign
Of God's Love, where we behold
Not black iron, hard and cold,
But white, red, and burning gold.

This you made and left no clue
By what name to pray for you.
You, I pray, ere long behold
White and Red, yea even Gold.
—Even the Rose's Heart of Gold.

THE OUTLAW

OI forgot that I was bound,
Forgot that I was shamed;
And I forgot I rode to death,
Because the sunset flamed.

The priest, who would have me repent
Beneath the gallows-tree,
Knows less of love than I who know
God has forgiven me.

Because I loved His fair green earth
and one pure heart loved me,
I too have known the Love of God
Who gives forgiveness free.

PRAISE IN THE WILDERNESS

BARE wilderness, you have grown fair to me.
The fragrance of the rose above the thorn
Endues me in the hour of ecstasy,
When through dark night I dream of radiant
morn.

To me you have been as the tombing earth
Is to the seed when darkness feeds desire,
Till longing quickens to the time of birth
And dust yields beauty to the informing fire.

O wilderness! Out of your barren ways
Are born immortal roses that our tears
Sustained in starless nights and flowerless days,
Through dense illusion of our mortal years.

Turn back again, you faithful who possess
The rose's guerdon! Pilgrims, turn again,
And cry, "Joy blossoms in the wilderness!
O brothers, leave the cities of the plain!"

PIERROT

O some there are who bury deep
   Lost joy in a grave far out of sight,
Saying, "O trouble me not, but sleep
In silence by day and night."

But I have left my joy to stay
Alive in the wood of my Delight.
Where the thrush and the linnet sing by day
And the nightingale by night.

But I—I wander away, away
Far down where the high road stretches white,
And I laugh and sign for the crowd by day
And weep for my heart by night.

I wait for the Morn when Death shall say:
"O come to the wood of thy Delight,
Where thy Love shall sing to thee at the day
And lie on thy breast all night."

THE OUTCAST

AN outcast mother laid her child
    Under earth's icy mould.
Her bitter cry froze on the wild
North wind: "How cold! How cold!"

God's angels drew that babe Love-blest
Out of the bitter storm,
And laid him upon Mary's breast:
"How warm!" she said, "how warm!"

THE DIVINE MOMENT

IN the dew-fresh fields of Dawn I wander,
Immemorial Immortal Dawn!
Far-off goal of man's most High Adventure
Whence our Dream, and whence our Hope,
   is drawn.

This the Garden of Celestial Blossom!
They who call me by my mortal name
Seem to me my captors and my gaolers,
In the strongholds of the House of Shame.

They who harshly call and bring me Earthward,
Draw my lips from Springs of Paradise!
Hope and Fear shall bind our lives together,
Love and Hate shall dim our mortal eyes!

In the fragrant far-off fields I wander,
O keep silence! Let the soul be free!
Let the soaring bird unscathed win Heaven!
Aim no arrow of mortality.

FLAME AND ASHES

TO hold a sword, keen-edged and
    battle-bright,
To weave a Spring-green garland for Delight,
To fight with Fate unfalteringly, and make
Surrender a vain word. For Beauty's sake
To enamel some white wall with bright dreams,
    set
Like gems in gold. Or cast a silver net
About strange words and fold them for men's
    eyes
As sweet enchanted birds from far-off skies
(So far they were but a passing note and gleam
Swift as the sigh that ends some lovely dream),
To draw embroidered curtains to the pale
Cold sky of Winter, having once cried "Hail!"
To the great Summer Sun! To lightly light,
And lightly quench, fierce torches thro' the
    night—
To kiss white lilies with parched lips that jest!
To wear a red rose on an ordered breast!

These things are fair,—or but those shielding
    masks
Which are the last gifts that the proud Heart
    asks.
Compassionate Death shall see what Life and
    Art
Found veiled,—the ashes of a ruined heart,
But kindlier Love, Lord of Dawn—lightening
    Lands,
Shall hold the Flame that burned it, 'twixt his
    hands.

TO X . . . WHO WROTE IN PRAISE OF MY HANDS

YOU made my hands a little hymn
    Of praise, calling them white
Beyond all hands—than all more slim
Acolytes of delight.

But would you learn the truth, these hands
Grew wan in floods of fire,
And worn with want in desert lands
Outstretched in vain desire.

Friend, when Death folds them on my beast,
Enshrine them in your art,
Calling them happy that they rest
Upon a heedless heart.

THE ROSE

FOR one short season of the year the Rose
Blossoms in radiant majesty set high!
Then the brief glory of the Summer goes,
And cold winds toss bare branches to the sky.

Yet through the tears of mournful Autumn
    hours,
Through barren Winter, and compassionate
    Spring,
Under fast-fading, bare, or quickening bowers
Our hearts still dream the Rose's blossoming!

The burning hands of lovers do but close
On some bright scattered petals of the whole,
Love not the lover holds the perfect Rose
In the immortal Summer of the Soul!

MARY MAGDALENE

OF all the Saints in the calendar,
 The most near unto the heart, I ween,
The quickest to hear and understand,
Is Saint Mary Magdalene.

And if Cain the Outcast prayed to her,
She would succour him with eager hand,
And tho' passionate Lilith would not pray,
She would help and understand.

DEW-TIME

LIFE gives us many spirits thro' the day
To laugh and fling flowers upon our way,
But at the end she gives us one to grieve
With our tired hearts that tears will not relieve—
    At Eve

Slowly the colours fade, the world grows grey,
And hopes and fears lie faded by the way.
Her soft tears all the meadows dew-drenched
    leave,
Shed from her heart for tearless hearts that
    heave—
    At Eve

And when the mystic dew-time fades away,
Dying with the last light I hear her say
Until dead hopes and flowers receive,
I will return and weep with you who grieve—
    At Eve.

THE DARK HOURS IN WILDERNESS

I LAY my face on barren sand;
     The thirsty sands drink up my tears,
My tribute to the desert lands
Where I have wandered years and years!

Insatiate sands, the whole world's flood
Of tears but leaves you thirsting still.
O could you drink of my blood
Your heart and mine had had their will.

Love holds the trembling mortal heart
Within the shelter of his hands,
And will not let its Dream depart
For all the drought of desert lands.

A CHRISTMAS LEGEND

"I'LL mourn no more that Winter days are long;
I'll build a fire and sing a song.
Perchance some wayfarer unseen by me
Shall hear my song and go more heartily.

I'll open wide the door—a table spread
With herbs and honey, and with oaten bread.
Perchance some wanderer shall see the light
And find goodwill, and shelter for the night."

So said an exile in a hut of clay,
Snow-shrouded, on the Morn of Christmas Day.
Rich merchants passed, and laughed to see
    coarse bread,
Wild herbs, and honey, for a Feast Day spread.

And king and courtiers gave him alms unsought;
But all the day no wanderer asked him aught!
Yet, though no outcast came his Feast to share,
He entertained an Angel unaware!

FOR A SEPULCHRE

B ETWEEN the hands, between the breasts,
    Down the white body 'twixt the thighs,
The sword is laid until it rests
Upon the once kissed feet. Men's eyes
Read "Odi et Amo" graven there.

Behind those eyelids now fast sealed,
Behind cold breasts that rose and fell
With passion, what has life revealed?
The great sword guards her secret well,
With "Odi et Amo" graven there.

O was it Love that conquered Hate?
Or was it Hate that set her free?
To Death all questioners come late;
The sword and the woman all may see,
And "Odi et Amo" graven there.

ROMANTIC LANDSCAPES

Evening

THE shadows lie across the field,
    The road in shadow lies;
The sun is gold upon the Earth
    And gold upon the skies.

The cavernous woods hold mysteries,
    The evening with hushed breath
Waits the harsh hoof-beats of my horse
    Upon the hill of Death.

High Noon

When gold was the green of the grass
    And purple the shadow of trees;
He watched in sweet pilgrimage pass,
    The joyfully labouring bees.

Watched dragon-flies' glittering gleam,
    Heard the reeds a soft lullaby croon,
And greeted Death's delicate dream.
    In the shadows that followed the noon.

RAIN

The grief of the grey evening lies
    Against the sorrowing slopes,
The huddled corn in longing sighs
    For all its long-held hopes.

We will go homeward, love, and rest
    And find our life more warm,
As, your head lying on my breast,
    We listen to the storm.

LEURNE, THE OUTLAW

IT was Leurne the outlaw—
    They hanged him on a tree,
Nor came there friend or maiden
To mourn him bitterly.

There, with cold hands behind him
And neck arye he swung,
And gaunt crows gathered round him
Till vesper bells were rung.

Grey monks passed by him slowly
And looked, nor was one found
To give him kindly burial
In consecrated ground

At moonrise came the tree-nymph,
And flung her arms around
His purple feet that starkly swung
An ell above the ground

And made great dole and weeping
Till, from the shadowy brake
Came thronging faun and dryad
A-sorrowing for his sake.

In the grey glimmering morning—
Just as the sun had birth—
The kind wood-people buried him
In God's most kindly earth.

FROM ROSAMOR DEAD
TO FAVONIUS
FOR WHOM SHE DIED

YOU loved my rounded cheeks!
    They have grown thin and white.
You loved my carmine lips!
They give no more delight.

You loved my flame-bright hair!
Quenched now its gleaming gold.
You loved my fragrant flesh!
'Tis waxen stark and cold.

But ah! the one thing, Dear,
You did not love in me,
Blooms soft, and red, and gold,
Fragrant immortally.

Not you, nor Time, nor Death,
Have any power to move
One crimson petal from
My perfect rose of Love.

Yet when death calls to you
The breath of Love shall part
The petals of my Rose
And bare its burning heart.

THE HARBOUR OF DELIGHT

HAPLESS the ship of fairest joy,
Plaything of Destiny!
There break no storms that may destroy
Her wraith,—Mnemosyne.

O, but her golden name I miss,
For in far days was she
Known by a fairer name than this
Sad name, Mnemosyne.

She now but o'er dream seas may glide,
I but dream havens find,
Till I go down to the dark tide
That leaves the world behind.

Spell-holden shall I step into
A waiting, mist-clad barque,
By strong cold winds be driven through
Dark, and still deeper dark.

Yet shall the light at last prevail,
The heart that held hope numb
Beat, as the emblems on the sail
Softly like voices come.

Then shall I leap unto the prow
And, bending downward, see
Storm-washed, mist-cleared, a name—but now.
No more Mnemosyne.

With quivering haste her bows shall break
Thro' seas that grow more blue,
I, who sailed dreaming long, shall wake
Within a dream found true.

The towers shall glow as if with fire,
Bright shine the sun, more bright,
Upon the land of my desire,
The harbour of delight.

The dead shall come down, hand in hand.
In welcoming pageantry,
Surging with hearts that understand
Fulfilment's ecstasy.

Then shall they bear me to a gate,
Fall back—and I shall be
Beyond the walls that baffle Fate,
Walls that encircle thee.

TREBLE SONG

TREASURE the golden moments as they pass
For Youth's a bird that flies too fast, alas!
Alas!
Treasure the rosy Dawn—too soon it goes;
Treasure the Morn—it fades, as fades the rose;
Treasure the Noon for it is hard to hold
Unstinted largess of Olympian gold;
And treasure Afternoon—
        that languorous thing—
For after Afternoon comes Evening.
And after Eve fast comes the dreadful Night
The tomb of all the golden Day's delight.
Oh, let us deck Apollo's shrine and move
His heart to give more gold. Oh, let us love
Thro' Dawn, and Morn, and Noon, and
        Afternoon,
For Love's the loveliest thing that goes too soon.
Dear Friend of all fair things that come and pass,
Fair Love's the fleetest of them all alas!
Alas!

THE FARM HAND

HOW Valour burns!
  With none to urge and very few to grieve,
He gathers up his scanty goods to leave
Slow toil of peace for the sharp toil of war.
With clay-stiff gait towards his uncertain goal,
Dreaming no fame, untroubled save for fear
They take his pride, the roan mare now in foal,
From harvest-fields in this great harvest year,
Across the wold beneath the pale first star,
Baring his wet brow to the evening wind,
No thought of his own valour in his mind,
To war he turns.
To war he turns.
Brother of warriors whose deeds outshine
Time's mists! From hearts like his where the
    Divine
Inviolable Fire has dumbly burned
Their honour soared! Finding no kindred spark
To leap from heart to heart—a running fire,
Theirs had been but a torch in the lonely night—

The flaming war-cry of a great desire—
A moment lifted—swiftly overturned.
God speed these Heroes as those Heroes sped!
Victory! Home! Or life with the great dead!
How Valour burns!

TO THE BAND OF SERVERS

IN ways that seem but dark and desolate
You lead with Light, O Souls of great Desire,
Lifting Day's torches till the blind who wait
In darkness see, and seek the Fount of Fire.

As Winds of Dawn, blown through the
    Wilderness
World-wards, you sing, till the deaf hear, and
    long,
And leave the silence, striving to possess
The Message and the Rapture of that Song.

Pilgrims of Love! who on the barren sands
Give your Heart's blood for those who faint
    and fail,
Into those emptied cups Angelic hands
Pour down the Treasure of the Holy Grail

THE BLESSED HEART

THO' Spring and Spring's full blossom,
    Summer, fade,
If Angus blest your heart be not afraid;
Tho' Spring's glad birds drop frozen at your feet,
His birds shall keep their heartsong still
    spring-sweet;
Within your heart shall burn the Rose's red
Tho' the earth freeze above your lying dead,
And you shall drink from streams of Paradise
When all the waters of the world are ice.

PARMA VIOLETS

PALE purple flowers, sweet lingering scent,
　　Magical violets—
Ah to what depths your message went,
Unloosed what winged regrets,

How swift across the silent years,
Across the sundering sea,
From night and rain of desolate tears
I come again to Thee.

Sharp from illusion drawn I see
How thin the veil of Death,
Whose mists fade melted suddenly
Before a flower's frail breath.

Cover my heart; hide tenderly
(Violet on violet)
My tears for fear the cold world see
All I would not forget.

THE DIVINE DISCONTENT

WHY are you vexed,
        O Soul, that your house
—Your house of clay—
No longer contents you?
O hasten away!
What do you here?
Does a tear,
Falling on dust, delay you?
Or a song stay you?
Cling not to Earth,
Rest not there,
When the land of your birth
Is so near.
Let not Body or Mind
With Fear or Joy bind
You down. Do you say
Still, "Alas for the Heart!"
That broken clay cup
From which the Divine
Life-giving Wine

Was offered up
Fouled with Earth's dust
For the lips of Love and the lips of Lust?
Grieve not, O Soul,
That the earthen bowl
Lies broken.
Its draught was but given in token
Of Living Springs.
Let not Earth bind your wings:
Haste you, O Soul, rejoicing, depart
From your house—your narrow house—
That no longer contents you.

THE SONG OF THE SEINE: TO THE COURT OF KINGS

"MY silver ripples wash away
   All madness from the brain of man,
In my cold darkness you shall surely say,
'Oh, but Death's arms are tenderer than
My lover's arms, wherein I lay.
Those arms from which you fled at last,
Shuddering through the night and day,
With maddened hands, that strove to cast
From out your life the fires that cling,
My depth can quench and heal, and low,
Long lullabies my sedges sing
To a heart that, beating upon a heart,
Slowly heard awful echoes there.
I will draw you to silence, so far apart,
Memory comes not, nor despair.

"And you, poor body, who once joyed so
In my city, and found it fond and fair
(Not even yet a year ago),

In royal state I will take you there:
Deaf to man's laughter and man's lies,
That is the royal way to go;
Cold to man's kisses, and with eyes
Too calm for tears or triumphs. Low
My courtier willows shall bow the head,
And proud, white clouds their shadows throw
Before the cold, triumphant dead.
O! Death's is a royal road to go.
And men in the city of your delight—
Glad city that once your laughter heard,
And the beat of your heart in the hush of the night,
Shall do your bidding without a word.
Without command they shall carry you where
Kings—conquerors of the world—keep state,
Whose courtiers do not even dare:
Speak to them—they are far too great;
With a conquered world beneath their feet,
Serene, indifferent, cold, they wait,
No voices can make those calm hearts beat,
Not even the voices of Love and Hate."

"Silver Singer!" the woman said,
"Would that you held me cold and dead;
But to do your bidding—then must I
Cast out Love ere I could die."

THE HOLY WAR

WE fight for Peace—not for Revenge or
        Hate,
Forgetful of the names of Fame or Fate—
Winning by war the Time when wars shall cease.
Soldiers of Concord! Sentinels of Peace.

FLOWERS

DELIGHT your eyes upon their beauty! Rest
   Your heart upon their beauty! Feed, O Soul,
Upon their beauty! Surely they are drest
More richly than King Solomon. No scroll

With blazoned letters and no clarion voice
Shall tell their Master's Will with more truth—
How He would have each child of Earth rejoice,
Serene from care, in an immortal youth.

The Sun shines on them, rains fall, and winds
      blow,
And they rejoice in winds, and Sun, and showers.
Why do you weep?—Consider how they grow.
Is not our life as lovely as a flower's?

Gather their gladness, Soul, and heart, and eyes,
To crown our lives: until we, ev'n as they,
Beloved of Beauty—Heirs of Paradise—
Abide to Joy, in the Divine To-day.

THE ORIFLAMME

WHEN with vexed heart and troubled
       mind
I sought the silence of the wood,
The low sheep-bell, scarce heard at first,
Called me softly from that mood.

It was not only the artlessness
Of sound that touched and healed my heart
Of all the subtleties of man,
And all the sophistries of art;

It called from out the distant past
A long-forgotten self, who went
With simpler heart and sane mind,
Singing across the downs of Kent.

It called me out to unspoiled youth,
It called me out to Spring's Delight,
It led me far through the dew-fresh morn—
Who went to meet the Winter night.

O that the heart of that old life,
Untroubled, happy, self-possesst,
Might overthrow this foolish heart
And beat again within this breast!

I know not now what joy I sought,
I know not now what joy I won,
Who followed that enchanted bell
Across the world to Barfreston!

I only know Delight was won . . .
That joy, unconquerable, keeps
His Oriflamme undimmed through all
The blinding tears dull Folly weeps.

And though the clouded heart and brain
Remember but a passing gleam,
I know in truth that Joy is Life
And Grief but the shadow of a dream!

THE LOVE OF CHRIST

THIS is the love our brother Christ . . .
     He crumbles the heart of clay
To treasure the few little grains of gold
Men threw away.

THE SWORD

LONG years ago the tender dawn revealed
    Softly a woman lying with lips sealed
By Death, and down her fair white body lay
A sword engraved—at length the perfect day
Shone upon "Odi et Amo" graven fair;
And the world's passing pageants wondered there,
And at last gave her burial in great state
There with her secret and her sword to wait

But the long years wear patiently away
God's and man's temples, be they stone or clay,
So the white body that held her heart
Crumbled to dust, and her tomb fell apart.
Then, with the coming, the high sun thrust
A golden ray deep down into the dust
That was that woman's and found there
A great sword, and all rust-eaten saving where
It had lain on her heart—Oh heart's desire!
It turned the word "amo" to flaming fire.

THE HEART-SHAPED SPACE
BETWEEN THE TREES

O heart-shaped, rose-filled space between
    The Trees of Knowledge and of Life,
In that delirious moment seen
When passionless peace is turned to strife
How fair before our eager eyes
The rose-bowered path from Paradise!

O Heart-shaped, thorn-filled space between
The Trees of Sacrifice and Pain,
So from the hither side is seen
The old land whereof our hearts are fain
How hard before those tear-blind eyes
The thorn-sharp path to Paradise!

APPENDIX

AT THE FORK OF THE ROADS

by Aleister Crowley

HYPATIA Gay knocked timidly at the door of Count Swanoff's flat. Hers was a curious mission, to serve the envy of the long lank melancholy unwashed poet whom she loved. Will Bute was not only a poetaster but a dabbler in magic, and black jealousy of a younger man and a far finer poet gnawed at his petty heart. He had gained a subtle hypnotic influence over Hypatia, who helped him in his ceremonies, and he had now commissioned her to seek out his rival and pick up some magical link through which he might be destroyed.

The door opened, and the girl passed from the cold stone dusk of the stairs to a palace of rose and gold. The poet's rooms were austere in their elegance. A plain gold-black paper of Japan covered the walls; in the midst hung an ancient silver lamp within which glowed the deep ruby of an electric lamp. The floor was covered with black and gold of leopards' skins; on the walls hung a great crucifix in ivory and ebony. Before the blazing fire lay the poet (who had concealed his royal Celtic descent beneath the pseudonym of "Swanoff") reading in a great volume bound with vellum.

He rose to greet her.

"Many days have I expected you," he exclaimed, "many days have I wept over you. I see your destiny—how thin a thread links you to that mighty Brotherhood of the Silver Star whose trembling neophyte I am—how twisted and thick are the tentacles of the Black Octopus whom you now serve. Ah! wrench yourself away while you are yet linked with us: I would not that you sank into the Ineffable Slime. Blind and bestial are the worms of the Slime: come to me, and by the Faith of the Star, I will save you."

The girl put him by with a light laugh. "I came," she said, "but to chatter about clairvoyance—why do you threaten me with these strange and awful words?"

"Because I see that to-day may decide all for you. Will you come with me into the White Temple, while I administer the Vows? Or will you enter the Black Temple, and swear away your soul?"

"Oh really," she said, "you are too silly—but I'll do what you like next time I come here."

"To-day your choice—to-morrow your fate," answered the young poet.

And the conversation drifted to lighter subjects.

But as she left she managed to scratch his hand with a brooch, and this tiny blood-stain on the pin she bore back in triumph to her master; he would work a strange working therewith!

Swanoff closed his books and went to bed. The streets were deadly silent; he turned his thoughts to the Infinite Silence of the Divine Presence, and fell into a peaceful sleep. No dreams disturbed him; later than usual he awoke.

How strange! The healthy flush of his cheek had faded: the hands were white and thin and wrinkled: he was so weak that he could hardly stagger to the bath. Breakfast refreshed him somewhat; but more than this the expectation of a visit from his master.

The master came. "Little brother!" he cried aloud as he entered, "you have disobeyed me. You have been meddling again with the Goetia!"

"I swear to you, master!" He did reverence to the adept.

The newcomer was a dark man with a powerful clean-shaven face almost masked in a mass of jet-black hair.

"Little brother," he said, "if that be so, then the Goetia has been meddling with you."

He lifted up his head and sniffed. "I smell evil;" he said, "I smell the dark brothers of iniquity. Have you duly performed the Ritual of the Flaming Star?"

"Thrice daily, according to your word."

"Then evil has entered in a body of flesh. Who has been here?"

The young poet told him. His eyes flashed. "Aha!" he said, "now let us Work!"

The neophyte brought writing materials to his master: the quill of a young gander, snow-white; virgin vellum of a young male lamb; ink of the gall of a certain rare fish; and a mysterious Book.

The master drew a number of incomprehensible signs and letters upon the vellum.

"Sleep with this beneath the pillow," he said, "you will awake if you are attacked; and whatever it is that attacks you, kill it! Kill it! Kill it! Then instantly go into your temple and assume the shape and dignity of the god Horus, send back the Thing to its sender by the might of the god that is in you! Come! I will discover unto you the words and the signs and the spells for this working of magic art."

They disappeared into the little white room lined with mirrors which Swanoff used for a temple.

Hypatia Gay, that same afternoon, took some drawings to a publisher in Bond Street. This man was bloated with disease and drink; his loose lips hung in an eternal leer; his fat eyes shed venom; his cheeks seemed ever on the point of bursting into nameless sores and ulcers.

He bought the young girl's drawings. "Not so much for their value," he explained, "as that I like to help promising young artists—like you, my dear!"

Her steely virginal eyes met his fearlessly and unsuspiciously. The beast cowered, and covered his foulness with a hideous smile of shame.

The night came, and young Swanoff went to his rest without alarm. Yet with that strange wonder that denotes those who expect the unknown and terrible, but have faith to win through.

This night he dreamt—deliciously.

A thousand years he strayed in gardens of spice, by darling streams, beneath delightful trees, in the blue rapture of the wonderful weather. At the end of a long glade of ilex that reached up to a marble palace stood a woman, fairer than all the women of the earth. Imperceptibly they drew together—she was in his arms. He awoke with a start. A woman indeed lay in his arms and showered a rain of burning kisses on his face. She clothed him about with ecstasy; her touch waked the serpent of essential madness in him.

Then, like a flash of lightning, came his master's word to his memory—Kill it! In the dim twilight he could see the lovely face that kissed him with lips of infinite splendour, hear the cooing words of love.

"Kill it! My God! Adonai! Adonai!" He cried aloud, and took her by the throat. Ah God! Her flesh was not the flesh of woman. It was hard as India-rubber to the touch, and his strong young fingers slipped. Also he loved her—loved, as he had never dreamt that love could be.

But he knew now, he knew! And a great loathing mingled with his lust. Long did they struggle; at last he got the upper, and with all his weight above her drove down his fingers in her neck. She gave one gasping cry—a cry of many devils in hell—and died. He was alone.

He had slain the succubus, and absorbed it. Ah! With what force and fire his veins roared! Ah! How he leapt from the bed, and donned the holy robes. How he invoked the God of Vengeance, Horus the mighty, and turned loose the Avengers upon the black soul that had sought his life!

At the end he was calm and happy as a babe; he returned to bed, slept easy, and woke strong and splendid.

Night after night for ten nights this scene was acted and re-acted: always identical. On the eleventh day he received a postcard from Hypatia Gay that she was coming to see him that afternoon.

"It means that the material basis of their working is exhausted," explained his master. "She wants another drop of blood. But we must put an end to this."

They went out into the city, and purchased a certain drug of which the master knew. At the very time that she was calling at the flat, they were at the boarding-house where she lodged, and secretly distributing the drug about the house. Its function was a strange one: hardly had they left the house when from a thousand quarter came a lamentable company of cats, and made the winter hideous with their cries.

"That" (chuckled the master) "will give her mind something to occupy itself with. She will do no black magic for our friend awhile!"

Indeed, the link was broken; Swanoff had peace. "If she comes again," ordered the master, "I leave it to you to punish her."

A month passed by; then, unannounced, once more Hypatia Gay knocked at the flat. Her virginal eyes still smiled; her purpose was yet deadlier than before.

Swanoff fenced with her awhile. Then she began to tempt him.

"Stay!" he said, "first you must keep your promise and enter the temple!"

Strong in the trust of her black master, she agreed. The poet opened the little door, and closed it quickly after her, turning the key.

As she passed into the utter darkness that hid behind curtains of black velvet, she caught one glimpse of the presiding god.

It was a skeleton that sat there, and blood stained all its bones. Below it was the evil altar, a round table supported by an ebony figure of a negro standing upon his hands. Upon the altar smouldered a sickening perfume, and the stench of the slain victims of the god defiled the air. It was a tiny room, and the girl, staggering, came against the skeleton. The bones were not clean; they were hidden by a greasy slime mingling with the blood, as though the hideous worship were about to endow it with a new body of flesh. She wrenched herself back in disgust. Then suddenly she felt it was alive! It was coming towards her! She shrieked once the blasphemy which her vile master had chosen as his mystic name; only a hollow laugh echoed back.

Then she knew all. She knew that to seek the left-hand path may lead one to the power of the blind worms of the Slime—and she resisted. Even then she might have called to the White Brothers; but she did not. A hideous fascination seized her.

And then she felt the horror.

Something—something against which nor clothes nor struggles were any protection—was taking possession of her, eating its way into her . . .

And its embrace was deadly cold. . . . Yet the hell-clutch at her heart filled her with a fearful joy. She ran forward; she put her arms round the skeleton; she put her young lips to its bony teeth, and kissed it. Instantly, as at a signal, a drench of the waters of death washed all the human life out of her being, while a rod as of steel smote her even from the base of the spine to the brain. She had passed the gates of the abyss. Shriek after shriek of ineffable agony burst from her tortured mouth; she writhed and howled in that ghastly celebration of the nuptials of the Pit.

Exhaustion took her; she fell with a heavy sob.

When she came to herself she was at home. Still that lamentable crew of cats miawled about the house. She awoke and shuddered. On the table lay two notes.

The first: "You fool! They are after me; my life is not safe. You have ruined me—Curse you!" This from the loved master, for whom she had sacrificed her soul.

The second a polite note from the publisher, asking for more drawings. Dazed and desperate, she picked up her portfolio, and went round to his office in Bond Street.

He saw the leprous light of utter degradation in her eyes; a dull flush came to his face; he licked his lips.

www.ingramcontent.com/pod-product-compliance
Lightning Source LLC
Chambersburg PA
CBHW050402110726
47899CB00008B/2618